GUARD HER WITH YOUR LIFE

A gripping crime thriller with a huge twist

JOY ELLIS

Joffe Books, London
www.joffebooks.com

First published by Audible in Great Britain in 2022

This paperback edition was first published
in Great Britain in 2024

Cover art by Nick Castle

ISBN: 978-1-83526-392-1

PROLOGUE

In the arrivals lounge of a busy airport, Sam Helsdown sat reading his ex-wife's letter. He'd been through it twice now, and it still didn't make sense. She had a 'situation', she said, and since he'd been pestering her for ages to let their daughter come and stay with him, now would be a good time.

What that particular situation was, he had no idea, and Julia had chosen not to enlighten him. For Sam, it couldn't have come at a worse time, the job being intense to say the least. But up to now Julia had always refused to let him see Zoe, so he was hardly going to refuse. Luckily, his boss had been through a difficult divorce herself and, knowing his situation, had cut him some slack and allowed him to take the leave he was owed.

Even though he was far too early, he kept his gaze fixed on the arrivals gate, wondering what Zoe would look like now. He hadn't seen her in two years, and kids grow up so quickly these days. She'd be ten now.

Two years gone, he thought bitterly. Two years of watching her grow, seeing what she would become. Two years of her life had been snatched away from him. It was theft on a grand scale, and it hurt.

He tore his gaze from the gate to the arrivals board and watched for the latest flight information. There it was at last, *Flight BA631 from Athens, Landed.* Oh Lord! Not long now.

He couldn't remember when he'd last felt so nervous. Sam didn't do apprehension, he did anticipation, enthusiasm, and a kind of zealous intensity when he was about to embark on some dangerous undertaking. All of which, after fifteen years with the Fenland Constabulary, was perfectly understandable. Getting the jitters was not in his DNA, and he found it quite unnerving.

He took a deep breath and pictured Zoe when he'd last seen her. A slender, petite girl with almost doll-like elfin features, pale blonde hair and blue-grey eyes. The image was etched into his brain. He smiled to himself. If ever there was a disparity between looks and personality, Zoe was the prime example. Her delicate features and small size masked a determination and strength that she'd manifested from the very day she was born.

Zoe had a mind of her own. She didn't suffer in the slightest from being an only child and having no siblings to interact with. She was an extremely well-adjusted little girl, happy both in her own company and with friends. Her confidence never seemed to waver. Far from it. In his daughter, Sam sensed an unshakable belief in her own capabilities.

He saw something of himself in the child, and he loved her the more because of it.

It was a busy terminal, in a constant state of flux, waves of travellers and staff shifting to and fro. The hurrying crowds made him almost dizzy. He liked action, but not this kind. The blind rush of people made him think of lemmings heading towards a cliff edge.

He shook himself, got up and went to buy a coffee. It would take a while for the baggage to appear and then to clear customs, although Julia had said Zoe would be travelling light. Even that had puzzled him. She was coming to stay for two or three weeks, and girls liked to have their things with them. A man living alone would have very little to offer in the way of clothes and the like, so he could see this visit being somewhat expensive. Not that he cared. He'd buy her the world if that's what she wanted.

Twenty minutes later, the first travellers toting cases on wheels began to filter through the doors, most of them inappropriately dressed for a January morning. Sam realised he was holding his breath.

The stream became a trickle. Where was she? He glimpsed a flash of pale blonde hair. Behind the rest, slightly obscured by a family fussing around three children and a case with a broken wheel, he caught sight of a slim girl in jeans and a blue sweatshirt. The girl was showing a photograph to a member of the airline staff who was escorting her, carrying the child's small cabin luggage case.

Zoe? His heart leaped.

The stewardess looked around. Her eyes fell on him and she smiled, pointing him out to the girl.

Head down, she ran towards him, and in moments she was in his arms. 'Daddy! Oh, Daddy! I was scared you wouldn't be here!'

He kissed the top of her head, holding her tightly. Finally, seeing the stewardess still waiting with the case, he held the child at arm's length so he could look at her properly.

An icy horror gripped him. The girl looking up at him so adoringly was not Zoe.

This was not his daughter.

CHAPTER ONE

Zoe, or whoever she really was, lay asleep in the bedroom he'd made ready for his daughter.

Sam sat opposite his brother, Mike, a bottle of whisky on the table between them. Each held a glass containing a lot more than a double measure.

'What the fuck is that woman up to this time?' growled Mike. 'I mean, it has to be Julia, doesn't it? Who else could it be? God alone knows what treacherous mess she's got herself embroiled in this time. It's beyond belief, it really is.'

Sam stared down at the passport lying next to the bottle of malt. It was in his daughter's name, her date of birth and other details all correct, but the face in the photo was that of the nameless child sleeping in the next room.

He was somewhat calmer now but still poleaxed, bewildered.

He had known intuitively that he must stifle his natural urge to scream at the stewardess, telling her this girl was not his daughter. Instead, he smiled and thanked her — not exactly a normal response to such an unbelievable situation, but then he and Julia weren't normal people.

Anyone else would have demanded to be taken to security, have insisted on calling the police. There'd have been urgent calls to the Greek police, to his wife, and a major hunt for his daughter would have been launched. The child with his daughter's name would have been taken into care, and efforts made to discover who she was and why she was here in the UK using a false passport.

Instead, the stewardess had returned his smile, saying that his little girl was a credit to him. Politely, she asked for his ID before she handed over her charge. He had shown her his warrant card, which was accepted without question. Returning it to his wallet, he had heard the child say, 'My Daddy's a policeman. I'll be quite safe with him.'

He took a long swallow from his glass and felt it hit the back of his throat.

Still rooted to the spot on the airport concourse, Sam knew as soon as she spoke that the child honestly believed him to be her father. What he didn't know was why. The story would have to come from her. It would require all his patience to extract it so that she remained in ignorance of the awful position they were in.

'What the hell are we going to do, Sam?' asked Mike urgently. 'For God's sake, someone out there is missing a little girl! And she's here, in your flat, tucked up in bed. In the eyes of the law — you, in case you'd forgotten — she's been abducted!' He took a gulp of his whisky. 'And who on earth is she?'

'She believes she is Zoe Helsdown,' whispered Sam, staring into his glass. 'My daughter. I don't know how the hell that has happened, but somehow I need to track down Julia — she's not answering her phone. Will you help me?'

'Of course I will.' Mike sighed. 'I'm sorry, mate, I'm just struggling to get my head around it. I really believed that when you waved goodbye to Julia, you'd be able to get your life back on track, and apart from wanting custody of Zoe, you could forget your psycho wife. Sorry, *ex*-wife.'

'Didn't we all,' lied Sam. The truth was that no matter where Julia went in the world, she would never totally let him go. And what he wasn't admitting to Mike was that a part of him still loved her.

'I don't know how you coped at that airport, Sam,' said Mike. 'I'd have freaked out.'

'I did, but luckily I kept it hidden,' said Sam with a rueful smile. 'There I was with a little girl hanging onto me who believed I was the father who had come for her. What would it have done to her if I'd called for security? And she had my photo clutched in her hand, Mike! As soon as I saw that, I knew it was something to do with Julia. And at that moment, all the bad stuff from the past came crashing back. I wanted out of that airport as fast as possible.'

'Did Zoe say anything?' Mike said. 'I have to call her Zoe, since we've no other name for her.'

'It's her name, Mike, as far as she knows, and we have to use it, even though it feels like a kick in the gut whenever I hear it. Poor kid was so knackered I got her a Happy Meal on the way home and told her to crash out. I said we'd talk in the morning.'

'Rather you than me,' Mike said.

'Actually, I can't wait. I need to know what the hell is going on, and where my real daughter is. This little kid is the key to it all.' Sam swallowed. 'She's all I have, Mike.'

'Not quite,' said his brother. 'There's me, and I'm going to find Julia for you. Question is, do you want her back dead or alive?'

But Sam wasn't laughing.

* * *

Sam woke at around three in the morning, covered in sweat. He'd been dreaming about Julia and it wasn't pleasant. He got up and went to the kitchen for a glass of water, but back in bed sleep still wouldn't come.

He lay staring into the dark, churning over old memories and trying to work out why Julia should send him a stranger in place of his darling Zoe. There were several reasons why she'd do such a thing, the most likely being that she'd done it to get her own back for something. She'd done it to mess with his mind.

He rearranged his pillows, trying to get comfortable. Julia was good at that. She could teach a masterclass in doing people's heads in, and he'd been her star pupil, gullible fool that he was.

He lay back, recalling their early days together. She was beautiful then, with the same pale blonde hair as Zoe, slim and lithe, and oh, how sexy! One look had been enough and he was hooked. From the first, Julia had been the one for him, a gorgeous, intelligent woman, an excellent police officer and the person he wanted to spend the rest of his life with. He'd fallen hopelessly in love with her, and he'd believed she felt the same. Until time proved him wrong. Despite all evidence to the contrary, he still clung to the belief that a part of her had loved him too, albeit a small part. But he wanted to believe that their daughter had been conceived in love. On bad days he was forced to think that Mike was right, that she had only borne him a child so she could use it against him one day. But when he recalled how good they'd been together in those first few heady months, he couldn't bring himself to believe it. But in that case, why had she given him a precious daughter to bond with and cherish for eight years, only to take her away from him? And she'd done it so clinically, like a surgeon with a scalpel, slicing through flesh.

Filled with pain and loathing, he contemplated the way his life had turned out. He'd been a quiet and dedicated police officer. A passionate affair with his new crewmate, Julia, had resulted in an unplanned child. He had wanted them to marry immediately, but Julia refused. She'd even decided they could no longer work together and had herself transferred out to another division. Despite his heartache and the endless struggle to hold on to his daughter, he had done well for himself. He'd been a bright and dedicated police officer who had risen to make detective sergeant. He was perfectly content with his life until Julia began to accompany

Zoe on her regular visits. She occasionally spent the night, and their relationship rekindled. This time she accepted his proposal of marriage, but continued to work elsewhere. It was a far from perfect arrangement, but they had managed, until Sam was temporarily transferred into a special unit, a Major Investigation Team dealing with a serious and high-profile crime. To his relief, the unit was eventually disbanded and he returned to CID. He had arrived in MIT to find himself teamed up with Julia again, and from that moment on, everything went wrong.

Now he regretted ever having accepted what had sounded like an exciting post. He regretted meeting Julia in the first place, but he didn't regret Zoe. She was the only good thing to come out of that whole mess, and even she had been stolen from him.

Trying to calm his increasing rage and bitterness, he turned his thoughts to the plight of the child who was now under his roof and in his care. Her situation was much worse than his. Apart from living a lie, which at some point she'd have to be told the truth about, why was she here at all? And was she in danger? He was a police officer and knew better than most why a pretty child might be smuggled in or out of the country.

Sam closed his eyes. He was exhausted, and he needed a few hours' sleep. Tomorrow was going to be difficult.

The hours crawled by and he couldn't stop his thoughts from racing. If this was indeed Julia's doing, for whatever reason, Zoe would at least be safe with her mother, but what if it wasn't Julia behind it? What if she'd crossed someone even nastier than herself and this was their work? And if this little stranger had been sent to him by some sinister unknown individual or group, what had they done with his daughter?

* * *

DI Terri Lander stomped back to her office, closed the door and leaned back against it, beathing hard. This was the second time this week that she'd crossed swords with the superintendent and she had a good idea it wouldn't be the last.

She went over to her desk and sank down onto her chair, swearing. She would dearly love to transfer out of this place and as far away from Superintendent Roger Clarke as possible. The Orkneys were looking pretty good right now. Whatever she wanted, whatever decisions she made, Clarke opposed, even when they were based on verified facts and figures. She'd come across men before who had resented women making their way up through the ranks, but Clarke left those others standing. Worst of all — apart from his chauvinist attitude — was that he wasn't even a very good policeman. Terri knew for a fact that he hadn't obtained that crown on his epaulet by merit alone. She, on the other hand, didn't need anyone to tell her what a bloody good copper she was. She worked hard and loved what she did, but Clarke was making it really difficult for her. That, of course, was exactly his plan. Roger Clarke had a man waiting to step into her office the moment she vacated it, and was doing all he could to speed up that exit.

Terri felt her face set in a look of grim determination. She was staying put, Roger Clarke or no Roger Clarke. Plus, she had no intention of moving to another station and leaving DS Sam Helsdown behind. He was the best sergeant she'd ever worked with, even if he did come with baggage, a lot of it, and had a past that left him open to all manner of speculation. All that meant nothing to her. No one was perfect, least of all her. She knew from experience that in their line of business, the first thing to suffer was marriages and relationships. Terri never passed judgement on people's personal lives. Love made fools of everyone at some time or another, and when love turned bad, it wrecked careers and split up families. As one who'd survived such a car crash, she was in no position to criticise anyone.

Today's battle had actually been about Sam. Unfortunately, she was aware that the super had a bit of a point when he'd questioned the wisdom of allowing Sam to take leave when they were deep in a serious investigation, but she'd refused to back down. Instead, she pointed out how much unpaid overtime he had put in on this case, plus the sick leave he should have taken but didn't. Then there were the outstanding holidays that were mounting up. In her opinion, it would be unfair to refuse him a couple of weeks out to spend with the daughter he hadn't seen for two years.

Terri had won the battle, but certainly not the war. It was exhausting trying to do her job, which was demanding at the best of times, and constantly watching her step so as not to fall foul of Roger sodding Clarke. The man was like some beady-eyed vulture, ready to swoop down and pick her bones clean if she made so much as one false move.

She certainly wasn't looking forward to a fortnight without Sam. He was her one ally — he hated Clarke as much as she did. It was good to have someone she could rant to and let off steam. Now she was alone, and just when it seemed Clarke was upping the ante. It was going to be a long two weeks.

* * *

While his unexpected visitor was still asleep, Sam went round his flat taking down all his photographs of Zoe and hiding them. It wouldn't do for the child to see portraits of a different girl adorning his walls and displayed on his bookcases. It'd be difficult enough trying to piece together what the kid had been told about him, and why she hadn't seen him before now.

He prepared them some breakfast, trying to quell his mounting rage. If Julia had put him in this terrible predicament, she had certainly stooped to a new low. And if it wasn't Julia? What then?

This had to stop. He really needed to get a grip and call on all his skills as a police officer. He was going to have to clear his mind of his feelings about Julia and what she might have done, along with all possible scenarios, and work only on what this girl could tell him. Somehow, he had to find out if she was in danger, and if that was the case, how to act. Mike had left late last night to prepare his search for Julia, so Sam was on his own for this.

He put out cereal and took milk from the fridge. Maybe it was best if he was alone. The second he had walked out of the airport with a child he knew not to be his, he had crossed a line. But as he saw it, he had no choice.

Sam took a deep breath. There was one person he dared share this with; the only one, other than his brother, whom he truly trusted. But there was no way he would jeopardise her career. It was precarious enough as it was, what with that bastard Clarke gunning for her. No matter what happened, Sam wasn't going to give that creep any extra ammunition to use on Terri. He'd have to face this mess without her. But it didn't make it any easier.

His phone rang, an unknown number.

'Yes?' he said warily.

'Don't speak. No time. Just listen.' The voice was urgent, staccato. 'I know what you're thinking, but you're wrong. Help will come. Until then, guard her with your life. It will be easier if you believe the child is yours. Just know she is priceless. Now. Call off Mike. Understand? Our Zoe is safe, but only so long as you do as I tell you. You are the only one I trust, Sam.' The call ended.

He stared at his phone, going over what had been said. Every word, every slight nuance in Julia's voice. *Help. Will. Come.*

Sam grabbed a pen and wrote down the message while it was still fresh in his mind. He stifled the impulse to hit return call and try to get back to her. It hadn't been a conversation, nothing was up for discussion, and it would have been no good anyway. It would never have connected, her phone either having been switched off or destroyed. He knew the drill.

However, he did ring Mike. He needed to do it before his brain started taking the unexpected message to pieces and began searching for hidden meanings, possible reasons for staging this whole weird charade. Plus, he could hear that Zoe was in the shower and out of earshot.

'Mike, listen. I'm not sure what your plan is but hold up.' He told his brother what had occurred.

'You're sure it was her?' said Mike suspiciously.

'As sure as eggs is eggs. It was Julia all right.'

'Then don't believe a word she told you. You know Julia, she's as trustworthy as a starving hyena. In fact—'

'I believe her, okay? End of. There was something in her voice, Mike, an edge. I don't have a sodding clue what is going on — more than I can even hazard a guess at, that's for sure — but it's serious. I mean it, Mike, don't risk my daughter's life. Do as I ask, and back off.'

Mike, he could tell, was unconvinced. Why should he be? He remembered the bad old days and what that woman had done to his brother.

'Think about it, please. I'm not sure how far you got last night in your search, but, hell, she's on to you already!'

'Not necessarily,' retorted Mike. 'She's no fool, she knows how you operate. You would turn to me first, get me to start a trace. When the closest person to you is a computer wizard with extraordinary skills and a hi-tech system better than the Kremlin's, it's only natural. And if she had picked anything up from me, with all the camouflage I throw around my searches, she should be running GCHQ!'

'And we can risk Zoe's life on that assumption, can we?' rejoined Sam coolly.

Mike groaned. 'Of course not, but for God's sake, don't take her word as gospel. She's got a serpent's tongue, which you know to your cost, as I'm sure you haven't forgotten.'

He hadn't. It still pained him, even after all these years. 'We need to talk, but not while Zoe might overhear. Unless you hear differently, come back tonight at around ten, okay? And in the meantime, please, please, no more searches!'

Mike sighed. 'Well, if that's what you want. But only until I manage to convince you that she's playing you for a fool. She's done it once, for fuck's sake, don't let her do it again.'

Sam pushed his phone back into his pocket. Mike was right to remind him about those terrible times, but for Zoe he'd go back there, walk into Hades and with a smile on his face.

'I'm sorry, Daddy, I overslept. Then I went and had a shower, I hope that's all right?'

The girl hesitated in the doorway, smiling uncertainly. Sam smiled back. Poor kid. He yearned for his own daughter, but his heart went out to the child who'd been caught up in all this. She looked younger than ten, although it's hard to tell at that age. 'Come in and sit down, sweetheart, you look like you need some breakfast.' He pulled out a chair for her. 'You and I have a lot of catching up to do, haven't we?'

She approached the table. 'I don't suppose you've got any hair straighteners, have you?'

He ran a hand over his cropped hair. 'Er, not my kind of thing, kid. But it might be a good idea to go shopping. Let's eat and then we'll make a list.'

CHAPTER TWO

Mike sat staring at his screen. He'd hoped this day would never come, but it seemed it had. At least he was well prepared for it. He knew exactly where Julia was, having tracked her passage around the world for over two years now. He glanced at a wall clock. At this very moment she was winging her way across Europe, heading for Edinburgh Airport.

Sam, of course, knew nothing of this, and Mike intended it to stay that way for as long as possible.

Mike Helsdown was the CEO of a large, well-known tech company. Time and again, he had begged his brother to join him, and if he'd done so, Sam would have been a much richer man than he was now, but oh no! Sam was going to be a copper and nothing else. That choice had brought him a heap of pain and heartbreak — not the career itself, Sam would always love that — but it had led him to Julia Berkman, and the destruction she had caused.

Mike hated Julia. He had every justification, given the way she treated his kid brother, but it wasn't just that. She had used Mike and his expertise to get what she needed. His business had a number of very important clients — individuals and organisations, including the police force, that required of their technology provider an extremely high degree of security and discretion. Her senior officers had assured him that she was a respected and resourceful member of an elite MIT unit and had their clearance to access sensitive information. On the basis of their recommendation, he had done a considerable amount of work for her in terms of technology. Oh, she was resourceful, all right. He was certain she'd used him to gain access to a lot more information than she'd shared with her unit. This she squirrelled away, probably to use for her own ends.

Needing caffeine, Mike left his office and headed for the coffee machine, deep in thought. How was he to save his brother from strolling straight back into the lioness's den while keeping his darling niece from harm?

He returned to his office and closed the door. He had tracked Julia unseen for all this time, and there was no reason for that to change now. He had in his possession some of the finest, most sophisticated software ever developed, including intrusion prevention systems that to the lay person would resemble something from a sci-fi movie. In turn, it would take a very clever mind to trace anything back to him.

He sipped his coffee. The only thing he could do was continue watching her virtually. His particular expertise might be needed more than ever now. Sam didn't want to make any ripples that could endanger Zoe, which was fine — nor did he — but it would be a big mistake to take their eyes off Julia. Ignorance was not bliss; it was bloody dangerous. And to prove the point, poor Sam believed her to be hundreds of miles away when, in an hour and a half, she would be landing on British soil. 'Yeah, bloody dangerous,' Mike muttered, and turned back to his monitor.

* * *

Over the years, Sam had taught himself to throw a switch that took him straight into work mode, a skill which might save his life or that of his team. It didn't come naturally to him. Like everyone, he was easily distracted, but a well-trained operative found a way to note any distractions and whether they represented a threat, and then either deal with them or disregard them. He had learned to do this while maintaining his focus on the primary objective.

He had not needed this particular skill since leaving MIT, but now he was glad of it.

He looked across the table to the child, who was adding a spoonful of blueberries to her cereal. He could see that he was going to have to modify his mode of operation in this situation. For instance, what he remembered of his real daughter might be relevant to how he dealt with this little imposter. Recalling such details might also keep him sane while he felt his way through this bizarre nightmare, like those patches of firm ground when you crossed a swamp.

Thus, he recalled that his Zoe didn't like blueberries. She called them the 'witch's fruit', from a book she'd read where a witch injected blueberries with a sleeping draught so as to render the handsome young hero powerless. This Zoe was adding a few more for good measure; she clearly loved them. He disregarded this. It was a small reminder of the reality of things, no more.

'I can't believe I'm really here,' said the girl, smiling shyly at him across the table.

'Neither can I,' he said truthfully.

She regarded him steadily. 'It must be really weird, meeting a daughter you've never seen before.'

Now that spoke volumes.

He looked at her earnestly. 'More than I can say.' He pushed his cereal bowl away from him. 'And since I know so little about you, that means I'm going to bombard you with questions. You'll just have to tell me if it gets too much, all right?'

'Sure. But can I ask you something too?' The blue-grey eyes, so reminiscent of his daughter's, looked directly into his. 'I don't want to upset you or anything — I know my real name is Zoe, of course — but the thing is, I've always been called Sophie, so do you think . . . ?' She gave a sheepish grin. 'I get kind of confused by being called Zoe.'

'I can handle that. Pleased to meet you, Sophie.' That simplified matters considerably. 'Know what I think? It would be really good if we had a real heart-to-heart so we could get to know each other, and then we can enjoy our time together and have some fun. What do you think? Where shall we start?'

'With that shopping list you mentioned. I really need those straighteners, Dad. No way can I go out looking like this!' She held up a swathe of wavy blonde hair, then dropped it disgustedly.

He obviously had a lot to learn. He reached for a notepad. 'Shopping list it is. We'll go to the big shopping centre on the main road into town, and what we can't find there we'll get on Amazon. It'll be here tomorrow. Toast?'

She said she'd love some, with some nut butter if he had any. Luckily it was a favourite of his too — he even had a new pot.

The shopping list turned out to be long, but eventually they were ready to go. Sam kept hearing Julia's words ringing in his ears: 'Guard her with your life.' He had every intention of doing just that. He wouldn't have chosen to go on this shopping expedition, but Sophie needed a lot more things than she had arrived with, and was not prepared to take no for an answer.

As it turned out, the shopping mall and garden centre was the best place for an excursion. The car park was out in the open, and it was busy, but not uncomfortably so. All he could do was keep the girl close, watching her and everyone around her like a hawk. Sophie was not a prisoner and he had no wish to make her feel like one. It was down to him to do as instructed and keep her safe, without scaring her.

It was a costly trip. If it had been his darling Zoe he was shopping for, he'd have thought nothing of it, but as it was, he vaguely wondered whether he might be able to claim expenses if he kept the receipts. He had no idea that a young girl would need so much. Even cosmetics, for heaven's sake. When did ten-year-olds start to use make-up and talk knowledgeably about nail art? At the biggest unit there, that of a well-known high street store, he arrived at the checkout to find she had collected a basketful of what she assured him were absolute essentials.

The assistant rang up the goods and presented him with the total. He swallowed hard, thinking of his credit card balance, and felt a tug on his sleeve.

'That's wrong, Daddy. She's overcharged you by nine ninety-nine,' Sophie said, absolutely certain of herself and not a little indignant.

'How do you come to work that out, Sophie?' he asked in amazement.

'I always add up what I spend as I go along. I was taught to be careful with my money.'

He looked apologetically at the assistant, who grudgingly cancelled the sale and rang everything up again. Then her face changed. She checked the two sales receipts against each other and exclaimed, 'Oh! I've scanned one item twice! I'm so sorry.' She looked at Sophie in awe. 'That's a very bright young lady you've got there!'

Sophie shrugged as if she'd heard it all before and it was no big deal.

Sam, on the other hand, thought it might be a very big deal indeed. 'You're good with figures?' he asked on their way out.

She nodded.

'Well, that definitely doesn't come from my side of the family,' he said with a grin. 'I struggle to remember telephone numbers, let alone tally my shopping up.'

Sophie said nothing. She seemed uncomfortable with the subject, even annoyed with herself. He came to the conclusion that she'd been told not to mention this attribute of hers, and now, on her first day with her 'father', she'd slipped up. He threw her a line. 'Hey, I meant to tell you at breakfast, you have an uncle, Mike, and he's really looking forward to meeting you.'

Sophie brightened immediately. 'That's nice. I suppose I've got a lot of relatives that I don't know about.'

'Not too many, I'm afraid. I come from a small family and most of them don't live round here. It'll all be a lot for you to take in at first. So we'll start with Mike — he's enough for anyone. He's a big guy, my brother, with a big heart to match.'

'I had a brother too — well, I called him brother because we were all part of the same foster family, but we were real good friends. His name was Costas.'

'Was?' Sam asked tentatively.

'He drowned.' She pulled a face and he couldn't quite read the emotion behind it. Regret, maybe, or was it annoyance?

'He had fits, so he wasn't supposed to go out fishing on his own, but he broke the rules. He fell overboard.'

They were on their way back to the car, loaded with bags. Sophie was still talking. 'He was so stubborn. He thought our foster mum and dad were being unfair on him because he loved fishing, so he went anyway and he died. How stupid was that? But then he was a boy.' She chuckled. 'Sorry, Dad.'

'Thanks, I'm sure,' he said.

Inside the car he felt easier. While they shopped, with Sophie chatting away, he had been constantly on the alert, watching the other shoppers for sudden movements, too much interest in them. Now he relaxed a little.

'You say you were fostered. Were they nice people? Kind to you?'

This time there was no mistaking the warmth in her voice. 'Sarah and Darius Lambros. She was English and Darius was Greek. They were lovely, and very kind to me. They brought me up. I miss them already.' There was a slight catch in her voice.

'I'm sure you do, honey. Hey, would you like to ring them when we get home, and tell them you're safe?'

Instead of looking relieved, she looked terribly sad. 'No, thank you.' She took a deep breath. 'Anyway, when I've straightened my hair, I'll tell you all about it. I don't think you've been told much at all, have you, Daddy?'

Sweet fuck all, actually. 'You're right there, Sophie.'

* * *

The Sophie who appeared for lunch was a different child to the one who had sat opposite him at breakfast. Straight blonde hair and the tiniest hint of make-up had added another couple of years to her age, and now he could see a suggestion of the beautiful woman this little girl would one day become. The subtle change in her appearance had brought confidence, too. Sam was impatient to hear what he hadn't been told, but reminded himself that he was dealing with a child. How much did she know or truly understood about her early life? What lies had she been fed? He might hear a whole web of them and still not know fact from fiction.

Sophie finished the salad he had prepared for her before she began. She regarded him seriously. 'I know they didn't tell me everything — adults don't tell children important stuff, do they?'

He nodded. 'That's true, but often it's to protect you. Adult stuff can be complicated and get confusing.' *Even for the adults.*

But Sophie wasn't to be fobbed off. 'Mainly it's because they think we're stupid and won't understand.' She started on her yoghurt. 'And some kids *are* silly, but you adults should recognise that some are not. I don't play with dolls anymore, I don't believe in unicorns or the tooth fairy, and I don't like being lied to.'

He agreed with her and said so. The problem was, he lied to her every time he opened his mouth. Suddenly he liked the position he'd been put in even less. 'Well, tell me what you know that I don't, and we'll try and make some sense of it.' He gave her a reassuring smile. 'And remember,

I'm a policeman, so I'll listen to what you say, but forgive me if I also ask questions, it's what policemen do.'

Sophie nodded. 'Well, I can only ever remember being with Sarah and Darius, although I know they weren't my real mother and father. We were all told we were fostered as soon as they thought we could cope with it.' She gave a dismissive shrug. 'It didn't matter to any of us, we were very happy and had a lovely home close to the beach.'

'Lovely home? As in comfortable? Small? Large?'

'It's a villa, with big gardens, and we all had our own rooms.'

'How many of you children were there?' he asked.

'Four of us.' She ate a spoonful of yoghurt. 'Until Costas died.' She was silent for a moment. 'Jim and Florence and me, we all felt exactly the same, like we'd been there for ever, but Costas said he had memories of being somewhere else.' She frowned. 'I think he had a . . . a vivid imagination, Dad. He said he remembered being kidnapped when he was very little, by men wearing masks and carrying guns. He said he lived in a big house in a city, maybe Athens — it was even bigger than the villa — and he reckoned that when he was old enough, he'd run away and find it.' She shook her head. 'But like I said, he was a boy, wasn't he?'

Maybe he was a boy with an actual memory, and now he was dead. Sam felt a shiver run across his shoulder blades. 'So,' he said quickly, 'you've lived all your life in Greece? Do you speak Greek?'

'*Milao aptaista ellinika.*'

He grinned. 'Silly question, wasn't it? Of course. You must be fluent.'

'I'm bilingual. Everyone in the house spoke both languages. Florence is the best. She taught herself French and German and even Albanian, and that's the oldest language in Europe, maybe in the world. She likes languages.'

'Clever girl! How old is Florence?'

'Twelve and a half. She's older than me, and she taught me lots of stuff about growing up.'

Ah, so maybe that's where the love of hair-straightening and make-up came from, he thought. *And was it a house of little geniuses, or a few impressive phrases picked up from tourists and seasonal workers? Most likely the latter.* 'And what is Jim good at?' he asked.

'Nothing much, he's just a nice person. He's very gentle and he loves animals, he's not like a boy at all.'

She had finished her yoghurt so he cleared the table and put the kettle on.

'Why don't you want to ring them, Sophie? After all, you were so happy there, and it sounds like Florence and Jim were like your brother and sister. Wouldn't you like to speak to them?'

She kept her eyes on the table. 'I'm not allowed to, Dad. We all understand that when we leave, we'll never go back. We move on to different lives and we start again.'

'And this Sarah and Darius, your foster parents, agreed to this?'

'Yes, Sarah told me that although they love us, all children have to part company with their parents at some point. Parents have to let their children go — they go off to get married, or their jobs take them far from home. She said she and Darius will always love us, but the time had come for them to send us on our way.'

At the age of ten? Sam doubted he could be so altruistic. But maybe the raw deal he'd suffered as a parent had coloured his judgement somewhat.

Seeing her sorrowful expression, he decided on a different approach. 'I'm making some coffee. Would you like one?'

She said she didn't drink coffee, but if he had chocolate, she wouldn't mind a cup.

They took their drinks into the lounge and sat on the sofa, side by side.

'So when did I come into the picture?' he asked.

'Julia tracked you down.'

He froze. 'Julia?'

'You know, Daddy! My social worker, the lady who found you for me.'

'I have a lot to thank her for,' he murmured, hoping he didn't sound too sardonic.

'We both do!' she said enthusiastically. 'And it took her ages after she saw your ad in the papers asking about me. Julia's amazing! I'd like to be like her when I'm older, except I don't think I'll ever be that clever.'

God forbid that she turns out to be anything like Julia!

'Anyway, Julia told me how I'd been snatched from my mummy when I was a tiny baby, and that Mummy disappeared too, and that you'd never given up trying to find me. Even though you were a policeman you never found out where I'd been taken.'

A tiny bell rang in his head. He'd heard this story before, hadn't he? Certainly something very similar. Then the penny dropped. Julia had used part of what had happened in the major investigation they'd been involved in, the one which went so badly wrong. *Clever Julia. Stick to what you know and there's less chance of making a mistake.*

'She said it took her over a year to trace us and make sure we really were related. Then she had to get the paperwork and stuff sorted, so that I could travel.' She gazed at him steadily. 'I know I'm only here for a little while, then they'll see how we get on. I mean, it's a big thing for you, taking on a kid, and a girl at that, but I hope . . .'

How was he supposed to deal with this? Julia had said he should try to think of the girl as his daughter, but how could he? Sam didn't have the heart to build up her hopes, but he could hardly tell her that as soon as 'help had come', he would most likely never see her again. He gave her the warmest smile he could muster. 'I guess it's a good thing. I mean, some people just don't get on at all, whether they're family or not. So I reckon we should just enjoy ourselves and face the music when the time comes.'

'Yes,' she said, 'and I think Julia might come over for the assessment. I'd like that. She's very beautiful.'

Sam kept the grin in place and quickly changed the subject. He seemed to be getting rather good at that. 'What was school like where you were?'

'We never went to school.' She stirred her hot chocolate. 'We had a private tutor, and Sarah home-taught us a lot as well. She's very clever. She made our lessons really interesting. She said school classes are too big, and no pupil gets the proper attention.'

'Oh dear. I don't think I'm really up to home-schooling, kiddo, unless you want to learn the Police and Criminal Evidence Act?' He pulled a face. 'Or I could teach you how to throw a controlled skid in a police car?'

Sophie looked at him reprovingly. 'I'm only ten, you know. Though the car one sounds like fun.'

One thing Sam had learned from their conversation was that when it came to these children, money was no object. Private tutors? Villas in Greece? For foster kids? Was that because someone wanted the best for them, or because they didn't want them in a school environment, out in public? If the latter was the case, was it because of possible danger, or because they didn't want the kids getting friendly with other children and their families?

'I wonder how you ended up in Greece,' he mused. 'How you came to be in such a wonderful foster home. I mean, a villa on the beach, it's idyllic.'

'Ask Julia. She knows, but she's never told me.'

'If she does come here, I certainly will,' he said with feeling. 'I'm afraid you'll find it very different here, angel — no beach, and not too much sun either. The misty Fenlands are a far cry from your Greek island. I hope you won't get bored.'

'Oh, I won't. They prepare us for it. Anyway, I have lots to find out about here, and you, and I have my homework to do as well.'

'You have homework, even though you've left your foster home and can't see your tutor?'

'Oh, Daddy! I can't believe they've told you so little. I'm going to tell Julia when she rings. It's really not fair on you.'

She looked quite sympathetic, which was strange for one so young.

'We have rules, you see. We know we've been very lucky to have been rescued and taken in, so we all promise to abide by these rules. It's a way of saying thank you. Doing homework is a way of saying thank you for being given an education.'

Sam was out of his depth. This sounded like oddest foster home in the world. He'd heard talk like this before, from kids who'd been indoctrinated into religious cults, and it gave him the creeps. He thought for a moment. 'Sophie, you do whatever feels right, but now you're here, we chill out a bit and get to know each other, and we don't need to follow any rules. I won't be checking up on you, so if you want to burn the rule book, you go right ahead and do it.'

Sophie looked horrified — or was she scared? Finally, she managed a smile. 'Okay, but I do enjoy homework, so I'll do that as well as chilling out, if that's all right?'

He held up his hands. 'Your decision. Do what feels right to you.' He frowned. 'But what do you do with your homework if you can't contact your tutor, or Sarah and Darius?'

Sophie got up from the table and went to her room, returning with a tablet. 'I send it off as soon as it's done. Then I get the next exercise to download. Simple.'

'But who sends it?'

She looked blank. 'I never asked. Some school or college somewhere, I guess. I thought it was how all home-schooling worked.'

He shrugged. 'Maybe you're right. I've never had anything to do with home-schooling. Nice tablet, and not cheap.' It wasn't. It looked like a very expensive one indeed.

'We all have one, just for schoolwork, nothing else.' She scrolled down and clicked. 'Oh good, it's more maths today.'

'That's one thing I've never said.' Sam made a face. 'Most other subjects were okay, but maths and I did not get along.' He looked at the screen and saw her latest assignment: "The Quadratic Function and the Quadratic Equation." His eyes widened. Shit! This was pure maths, probably sixth-form level. Who was this kid?

CHAPTER THREE

'Do you think you could make it a little earlier, Mike? Then you can meet Sophie before she goes to bed.'

'Sophie?'

'Stroke of luck, there,' said Sam. 'I'm not sure if it's her real name or was given to her after she was fostered as a baby, but it makes it all a whole lot less painful for me.'

Mike said he could get there at about nine. Having reminded his brother to act as if this little girl was his niece, Sam hung up.

It was after seven now. Sam thought back over the strange day he'd just had. Part of it had been spent online, buying Sophie more new clothes. He guessed that this had been the best part of the day for ten-year-old Sophie. It would have cost him even more, but she seemed to prefer the cheaper, trendier range sold by the big supermarkets. Apart from wishing he could be doing this with his real daughter, Sam found that he was enjoying himself just watching her excitement at each new purchase. He noted that despite not believing in unicorns, a vivid pink sweatshirt had made its way into her basket, which bore a logo featuring that very horned beast. Given the chilly Fenland weather, he himself added an expensive pink padded jacket with a faux fur trim around the hood. He asked her why she had arrived with so few belongings, to which she answered reasonably that she was travelling alone, and they didn't want her worrying over numbers of heavy cases. Anyway, she said, it was a trial period. If all went well, her things would be shipped over. If they did not go well, they'd be sent elsewhere. Tentatively, he asked if she knew where. Probably a different foster home, she said, but still in the UK, or maybe even the States. She had looked a little desolate then, so he had done what he did so well these days and changed the subject.

Right now, Sophie was flicking through the channels on his TV, giggling in delight. She said they rarely watched television at the villa, and were never allowed to choose the programmes. Darius always selected programmes he considered suitable for them. It was so cool, Sophie said, being able to work the remote herself. After some deliberation, she was now immersed in *Frozen*.

Sam took the opportunity to make notes on his laptop. He wasn't sure how sensible this was, not knowing the severity of whatever he was caught up in, but he needed to make a record of some of the things Sophie had mentioned in passing. He had no idea if they were important, but they would at least help him build up a picture of the child and her circumstances. What, he wondered, would it show?

Mike arrived punctually at nine. The epitome of a doting uncle, he had even thought to bring a box of chocolates and a cuddly teddy bear for Sophie, which clearly made him a legend in her eyes. She might not play with dolls, but bears were obviously most acceptable.

Watching them together, Sam thought Mike was much better at this than he was. But Mike would be going home before long, whereas he had to manage Sophie all the time.

They gave Sophie a good half an hour to get to sleep, with Sam listening at her door to hear her breathing slow, before they discussed anything. Even so, they spoke in lowered voices.

Sam spent some time filling his brother in on what he had learned so far, including the approximate location of the foster home in Greece.

Mike looked puzzled. 'It's a very odd set-up, I must say. No school? I mean, how do the kids learn to socialise?'

'It's more than odd, bro. I could be wrong, but she alluded to boundaries, security too. It made me think of a compound — luxurious, but still strictly controlled.'

'Sounds more like a gated community to me,' Mike said. 'A bit like those tourist hotels in dangerous places like the Dominican Republic. In any case, those children were kept in very different conditions to those of normal orphans in foster care.'

'I think the children themselves are different,' said Sam slowly. 'What would you say if I told you Sophie was happy to be sent maths homework, and not only that but pure mathematics to at least sixth-form level?' He told Mike about the cashier overcharging them.

Mike whistled softly. 'A genius? Is that what you're saying?'

'I don't know about that, not being one myself. But her brain seems to work like a calculator, only faster. Oh, and she's not keen on talking about it, although she did say that one of the other kids, a twelve-year-old, taught herself French and German and, wait for it, Albanian! She could have been exaggerating, but the more I see of Sophie, the more I think she was telling the truth.'

'And now that remarkable little brain, having been heavily protected and cossetted for years, is in your spare room in a two-bedroomed flat in a dreary Fenland market town.' Mike blinked several times. 'Is it me? Or can you smell something really off?'

'I'm telling you, Mike, the scenarios my mind is coming up with are the stuff of nightmares. For God's sake, Julia told me to guard her with my life! That this kid is priceless! What exactly has she dropped me in?' He rubbed his eyes with his fists. 'I've told Sophie we must have some fun, but what can we do? Where can we go? Any moment a car could draw up, and men in hoods leap out, cosh me, bundle her inside and drive away. Yeah, and all the time I have to keep up this bloody awful lie that I'm her father! This is an impossible situation.'

Mike let him rant for a while, then said calmly, 'I think we need to invent a new situation, don't you? Think about it. If Julia can use you, you can use her too.'

Sam felt his blood pressure return to something like normal. 'Like how?'

'I'm thinking something along the lines of . . .' He paused, frowning. 'Okay. You've had a call from Greece, someone you assumed to be Julia, but she was very secretive. There has been a threat of some kind, and until they understand what and who it concerns, you and Sophie need to be vigilant. Don't over-egg the pudding, and don't scare her, but it would give you a bit of leeway to lay low and play Scrabble or take up diamond art, rather than sightseeing or looking for the nearest Go Ape park.'

Sam thought about that. 'Could work. She's very enamoured of Julia, so she'd go along with whatever she said. However, she said she does get calls from Julia, so what if she mentioned it and Julia denied it?'

'You only said you *assumed* it was Julia.'

'Mmm, and Sophie said herself that Julia doesn't tell you everything. Yeah, that could work.' Sam nodded slowly.

'And save you a whole lot of worry.' Mike considered his brother. 'You might not like what I'm going to say, but I have to say it. As a police officer, I'd happily trust you with my life, but in the matter of your relationship with Julia, you don't know your arse from your elbow. In a call that probably lasted about twenty seconds, she's managed to convince you of every word she said. As a consequence, you've landed yourself in deep shit. You've put your job, the career you've given your whole life to, on the line, all because yet again you've jumped the moment that bitch clicked her fingers.'

Sam could hardly argue. 'Right on all counts but one. I jumped the moment I heard that my daughter was in danger.

Bad judgement or not, I'll not risk Zoe at any cost. And you didn't hear how she spoke, Mike. I promise you, Julia was in deadly earnest. Zoe's life comes first, over my job, my reputation, my friends, even over my brother.' Sam smiled wryly. 'But regarding the last, only if it comes right down to the wire, of course.'

Mike shook his head. 'I really hope it doesn't, but I'll not be placing bets after what you've been telling me about Junior Mastermind in there.' He jabbed his thumb towards the bedrooms. 'Sounds like she could be hot property.'

'Whatever she is, she's still a little girl,' said Sam. 'And blissfully unaware that she's sitting right in the eye of a storm. Maybe someone somewhere is feeling the same as me, not knowing where his beloved daughter is, or if she's safe. The only thing I can do for her is protect her. I think that's what Julia meant when she said it would be best to try and think of her as my own. If I can do that, maybe someone else will do the same for Zoe.'

'Ah, the law of karma — cause and effect,' murmured Mike.

Whether he'd said that out of reverence or scorn, Sam wasn't sure. He opted to believe the former.

'All right. So I must back off, but I can't just sit and do nothing. I need to help in some way. What do you suggest I do?' Mike asked.

Sam thought about it. 'Don't make waves. Don't let Julia, or whoever she's working with — or even against — find you poking about in their personal cyberspace. Though you might use that amazing talent of yours to carry out a discreet search into missing British children — girls of Sophie's age, possibly snatched as infants. She said she has no memory of being anywhere other than Greece, with her foster parents, so whatever happened to her, it was done when she was still a babe.'

'No problem,' Mike said, 'and believe me, no one will know what I'm doing. How about the other kids? The ones who were with her in that foster home?'

'No, definitely not,' Sam rejoined. 'Far too risky. We have no idea what kind of cyber protection they have. If those kids are as important as I'm coming to believe, we leave well alone. I know you're the best there is, but we have no idea what we're dealing with, or why those children are there. Take no risks, okay? Think of Zoe.'

'Okay, I'll stick with Sophie.' Mike looked at his watch. 'I'd better be going. Listen, from now on I'm going to check in with you twice a day, just to be on the safe side. This whole thing is giving me the willies.'

'That's good by me, and maybe you could call round for an update sometime.'

After Mike had left, Sam thought of something he would have loved to get his brother to check, but he didn't dare. He kept thinking about the rules Sophie had spoken of, and how you didn't break them. But one boy had. A boy called Costas who still retained a memory of his previous life. Costas broke the rules and died. Was that an accident? Or punishment?

* * *

Outside in the street, Mike started his engine and drove away. At the same time, a second car pulled out and followed behind him. As they left, another car slid into the vacant parking space. The driver switched off the ignition and settled into his seat, ready for a long night.

* * *

Mike had intended to go straight home but Sam's request had whetted his appetite. Keen to begin his search for girls that had gone missing around ten years ago, when Sophie disappeared, he decided that his office was the best place to start. So he drove to the small business park outside town where his firm was located.

MH TEC Services occupied a modern three-storey office block which also housed a Samaritans call centre, an

NHS hub that dealt with the coordination of community and night workers, and a mail order company that operated a twilight shift from 8 p.m. till two in the morning. Thus, anyone seen working late at MH TEC wouldn't look out of place. There was always someone manning reception and a security guard patrolled the building. Rather than drive to his own parking spot at the side of the building, he parked out front in the visitors' bay.

'Evening, sir,' a chirpy voice said as he went in. 'Couldn't you sleep?'

Mike grinned. 'Hello, Ricky. Something like that. I should only be an hour or so. I'll give you a shout when I leave, okay?'

The young man touched an imaginary peak in an informal salute. 'See you later, sir.'

Mike unlocked his office and turned up the lights. Within minutes he was deep into his search. He had been working — unsuccessfully — for about half an hour when there was a soft tap on the door. Ricky stood in the doorway. 'Sorry to interrupt, sir, but someone left a letter for you.'

Mike went to take the envelope from him. 'Thanks, Rick. Bit late for callers, isn't it?'

Ricky nodded. 'She said she was passing by on her way home from somewhere. She had intended to put it in the mailbox for you but I said you were here so I'd run it up to you.' He gave his customary salute and strolled back down the corridor.

Mike returned to his desk and opened it.

> *Have a care, Mike. This could have been a letter bomb. It isn't this time, but as you are hell-bent on ignoring your brother's warning to back off, perhaps you will listen to mine. Just go be a brother and an uncle, and not some shadowy avenger, understand? Oh, and if you think you needn't take this seriously, take a look outside your window.*

Cautiously, Mike went over to the window and looked out.

The car park was quiet. There was a good scattering of cars belonging to the twilight shift and the night workers, but it was far from crowded. No one was out there walking around. Nothing. Stupid, he told himself, standing here searching the darkness for hidden danger. He was about to turn away when he heard a *whoosh*, followed by a loud crack, and his vehicle burst into flames. In moments it was ablaze, car alarms were going off, and already he could hear shouts from the other offices.

Mike stood frozen to the spot. He stared at the letter still clasped in his hand and swallowed hard. Then he heard someone yelling out his name.

'Mr Helsdown! Your car!' Ricky, white-faced, was calling to him from the doorway. 'The fire service are on their way and Arnie's getting the other people to move their cars to safety. Dunno what the hell happened, sir, but your car's a goner!'

Mike tried to fight off growing panic. Fire service meant the police, which was the last thing he needed with everything that was going on. He folded the letter and plunged it into his pocket. 'I . . . I saw it go up! Er, I'll be right down, Ricky. You go and look out for the fire engine.'

As soon as Ricky had hurried away, Mike rang Sam, blurting out what had happened.

'Act shocked, Mike! Tell them you have no idea who could have done it. You've no enemies in the world and all that. You know the score. Make them believe it must have been random. Ring me when you're clear, okay?'

It was all he could do. He just hoped they'd believe him.

When he got downstairs, the car park was like a scene from an action film. People were rushing to get their own vehicles as far away as possible, and a few brave souls, including Arnie, the night security guard, had grabbed office fire extinguishers and were trying to prevent the fire from spreading.

Any minute, Mike expected to see his car explode but Ricky, who was standing next to him on the reception steps, knowledgably informed him that outside the Hollywood movies, it was very rare to see a car actually blow up.

'They can flare up, especially if a tyre blows and blasts air into the fire, and they can burn completely out, Mr Helsdown, but *boom*? Nah. Unless they're an electric car that uses over six thousand lithium-ion cells. I wouldn't trust one of those babies.'

Mike vaguely wondered where all that information came from. Then he recalled that Ricky's car was a bright red Mazda MX-5 Miata, and realised he was talking to a petrolhead.

The fire engine finally roared into the park in a blaze of lights and the screaming of sirens. The response time had been around eight minutes. While they worked on controlling the blaze, Mike saw a police car swing in and stop in front of the building. His heart sank.

After exchanging a few words with the fire officers, the two uniformed constables headed for Mike.

'This was your car, sir?' said one of the two women PCs, pointing towards the burnt-out Toyota.

Was. That car had been his pride and joy, and worth forty thousand pounds to boot. He nodded.

'Have you had any trouble with it recently? Any warning lights? Loss of power?'

'No, nothing at all, it's — it was — a really reliable car.'

'Well, we can't blame this on someone doing a bit of dodgy DIY wiring then, can we? Looks like vandalism or arson, I'm afraid.' She gave him an apologetic smile. 'We'll need some details from you, sir. Shall we go inside?'

They sat in the reception area. The officer introduced herself as PC Ginette Taylor, and asked him his name.

'Hey! You must be Sam's brother.' She smiled at him. 'Good bloke, Sam. I worked with him before he went off to CID. Give him my best, won't you?'

He said he would, then gave her his address and contact details, and managed to act both shocked and angry at what had happened.

'So there's no one you can think of who might hold a grudge, sir?' The other officer didn't seem quite as friendly as Ginette. 'Only it appears that it was your car in particular that was targeted.'

He shook his head, saying he hadn't even the slightest idea who could wish him ill.

'Was there anything of value locked inside the car, sir? I assume it was locked?' The second constable fastened him with an unblinking stare.

He thought about that. 'I left nothing in it of value, just the usual junk you stow in the boot, you know, wellies and all the car stuff — scrapers, a blanket, hazard triangle and a tyre pump.' He pulled a face. 'I think I locked it, but my mind was on work, so I could have forgotten.'

'And there's no chance this might be connected to your brother?' asked Ginette suddenly.

The question shook him. 'You mean, as in trying to get back at a police officer for something? Like someone he's upset or arrested?'

She shrugged. 'We're fair game for some members of the criminal fraternity, I'm afraid. Although it's not usually this radical. Maybe we should have a chat with him?'

Mike knew he had to do something, and fast. 'Give him a break, PC Taylor. He's got his little daughter come to stay with him for the first time in years. Don't bother him with my troubles. Tell you what.' He mustered his best smile. 'How about I have a quiet word with him, well out of his little girl's hearing, and then I get back to you?'

'Sure.' She took a card from her pocket and handed it to him. 'As soon as you can, if you wouldn't mind.'

He could have cheered. It seemed he was a better liar than he thought.

'We'll liaise with the fire boys,' she added. 'They'll most likely be able to tell us how it started, then we need to decide who is responsible for removing it. We'll only do it if we have to take it for forensic evidence. Otherwise it could be down to the council or whoever owns the car park here. Meanwhile, Jo and I will take a look at the CCTV. You never know, we might have caught some little scrote red-handed.'

Rather doubtful, thought Mike grimly, *but please do go ahead*. He gathered from what she had just said that he was going to finish up with a hefty haulage bill from someone. Well, he'd pay up as soon as possible if he thought it would bring a swift end to this whole damned drama. Oh God, and he needed to notify his insurance, too. He rubbed his temples, feeling the beginnings of a mammoth headache.

While the police liaised with Arnie about the security cameras, Mike went up to his office to look for paracetamol. He took two and sank down at his desk, the real, gut-wrenching worry setting in. He would have put serious money on his system being absolutely foolproof. No one could possibly hack into it, so how come Julia knew about the search he was doing? Having thought long and hard, he came back to his original conclusion. She didn't. But she did know how close he was to Sam and that he'd do anything for him. So the warning was based on her assumption of how he'd act if Sam told him what was going on. Well, her guess had been accurate to the nth degree.

He took the note from his pocket and stared at it. He couldn't recognise Julia's handwriting, but Sam would. He was surprised it hadn't been typed, but she clearly wasn't bothered by him knowing who had sent it.

'Mr Helsdown, sir.' Ricky was back. 'The police want you to take a butchers at the CCTV with them. They've spotted the bird that delivered your letter. I've IDed her as the messenger all right,' he said rather proudly. 'Can you come?'

'Of course. I'll just get my things together and lock the office.' He sounded calm, but inside he was panicking. The police knew about that bloody letter! Oh shit, shit, shit! Then, in a moment of clear-headedness, he scanned the letter and sent it to Sam. He then put the original, and the envelope it came in, through the shredder.

Back in the foyer, he tried to look composed.

'We understand that this woman brought you a letter just before the car was torched, Mr Helsdown. Can you tell us what it concerned?' Ginette sounded very suspicious.

'That! Oh no, that was from a business friend of mine. He'd recommended me to a prospective client I sent some quotes to and the note was thanking me. I have no idea who the woman was, though. Maybe his secretary, or a relative was passing this way and dropped it in?'

'Take a look at her, please. Maybe you'll recognise her.' She pointed to a blurry image on the screen.

He prayed he wouldn't be able to. And he couldn't. It might have been Julia, he supposed, but it didn't show her face, just a side-to-back view, so he honestly couldn't say. He shook his head. 'It's not exactly clear, is it? But I'm pretty sure it's no one I know. Sorry.'

Ginette still looked dubious. 'I don't like the way she comes into reception, goes out a minute or two later, but it's over three minutes before we see her again walking out of the car park exit. Where was she for those three minutes?'

Mike swallowed hard. *Yeah, where was she?* 'Surely, if you can see all this, can't you see my car and who was tampering with it?' he asked a little testily.

'We could, if there wasn't a high-sided vehicle pulled in between the security camera and your Toyota for that exact time frame, sir. Rather convenient, wouldn't you say?'

She ran the video again, and he saw a big white van drive in, pause for a couple of minutes, and then drive out again. The plates were not visible. He murmured, 'Yes, Officer, I see what you mean. My car really was torched on purpose, wasn't it?'

''Fraid so, and we are going to need that letter, and your business associate's contact details. The woman might have nothing to do with it, but—' Ginette didn't finish the sentence.

'Oh no!' he groaned. 'I stuck it in the shredder! It wasn't anything important. I shred all my old memos and unwanted bits of paper and printouts, it's a habit.'

'And your colleague?'

'Of course. His name is Jack.' He rubbed his forehead. 'Look, can we do this in the morning? I've got a cow of a headache, and there's so much to sort out, beginning with a hire car. Hell, I've lost my vehicle to some bloody fire starter!'

Ginette relented. 'Yes, sir. Can you come into the station tomorrow morning? Or would you like an officer to call at your home? It has to be done as soon as possible, I'm afraid.'

'Yes, yes, I'll be there,' he agreed. One thing was for sure, he didn't want them turning up at his home. 'Give me time to sort some transport, say eleven, that okay?'

On hearing that eleven was fine, he turned to Ricky. 'Ring for a cab, lad, would you? I think this is turning into a migraine. I need something stronger than paracetamol.'

* * *

It was after midnight when the taxi dropped Mike off at his home. The first thing he did was make a phone call.

'Hi, Jack. I'm guessing you're awake, but are you sober? I've got a big favour to ask.'

Jack Horton laughed. 'Awake, semi-sober, and I've been doing you favours since we were six. What is it this time?'

Mike hated not being able to tell his oldest friend exactly what was happening, but he didn't dare. 'You're going to have to trust me on this, mate. Er, it involves the police.'

Jack's laughter died away. He sighed. 'What do you want me to do?'

'If the police contact you, can you confirm that you're a friend and business contact of mine. Emphasise the business part.'

'Sure, and what else?'

'Yesterday you wrote me a note thanking me for sending some quotes to someone you recommended. You had intended to either give it to me if you saw me, or drop it into the office as you live nearby, but you must have dropped it somewhere, because when you got out of your car it had gone.' Even as he spoke, his story sounded pretty lame.

'Let me get this straight,' Jack said. 'I wrote you a thank you note, but you never got it? What's the point of that?'

'I did get it. It was brought to the office by a woman. It was a rather, er, difficult note to explain to the police for a reason I really dare not talk about. I shredded it, now they want to confirm that you really did send it.'

Jack was silent for a few moments. 'So I drop the note and a kindly soul picks it up and takes it to the address on the envelope.'

Mike groaned. 'Shit, that's not going to work. She told the receptionist she was just passing and brought it in.'

'Nothing wrong with that, is there? She could have meant she took it in herself rather than stick a stamp on it. And anyway, the moment I confirm I wrote the letter and probably dropped it, the police won't take it further.' Jack chuckled. 'And what *was* this letter from a mystery woman, you sly old fox? Carrying on behind her husband's back, are you?'

Why not? thought Mike. It wasn't his style, but it happened. 'Let's just say it's serious. Jack, someone torched my car.'

'Bloody hell, mate! What have you got yourself into?'

'Please don't ask. I promise I'll tell you when I can, but not yet.' Then he added, 'Look, mate, I've done nothing illegal, except for lying to the police. So you'll not get mixed up in anything crooked, I swear.'

Jack again went over exactly what he was to say. 'I can't wait to hear the outcome of all this, but in the meantime, good luck, my friend.'

He was about to hang up when Mike remembered something. 'The new client! The one you "recommended". They could ask for a name.'

Jack grunted. 'Have you sent out a quote to anyone recently?'

'Er, yes, earlier yesterday morning. A Mr Lewis. Brian Lewis.'

'Then Brian Lewis it is. Just in case. And while we are on fail-safes, why didn't I just text or email you?'

'Because you're an old-fashioned sort of guy, I guess. Your mum taught you good manners.'

'My mother wouldn't have given a flying fuck for manners, as you well know. What a load of crap! But as I can't think of anything better, we'll have to go with that. Now go and get some sleep, you sound like you're running on empty.'

Mike breathed again. This lying was a complicated affair.

CHAPTER FOUR

The later it got, the more anxious Sam became. He sat, a small whisky in his hand, and stared at his mobile. It was after half past twelve when his brother phoned him. At the end of the call, he was even more worried. He wished to hell that Mike hadn't started lying to the police, but what else could he do? Sam had read the scanned letter that Mike had emailed to him, and it was far too damning to keep hold of.

Sam padded back to his bedroom and climbed into bed, but sleep wouldn't come. Part of him was pleased that it had been Ginette Taylor that had turned out for the car fire — she had been a good mate way back — but her crewmate, Jo Greene, was noted for her terrier instinct. Jo could smell a rat at forty paces. That could be a worry, because he wasn't sure that Mike, a basically solid, honest bloke, was up to becoming an accomplished liar.

Then thoughts of Julia flooded his brain, at which even the slightest vestiges of sleep left him. Mike had said a woman had delivered the letter and had been in the car park just long enough to torch his car. The tone of the warning certainly indicated that she had been the source, but if she had delivered it personally, she had to be here in town, not in Greece. He recalled her words, 'Help will come.' Did that mean Julia herself? He wondered what he would do if he ever saw her again face to face. Mike had been right, although Sam would never admit it to his brother. She was the one thing that he did not trust his own judgement on. Becoming involved with Julia was the only time in his life that his heart had overruled his head, his gut, and his common sense.

Sam closed his eyes, hoping against hope that help *would* come, and soon, and in the guise of a team of altruistic helpers, all there to return a little girl to her rightful home. He also hoped that Julia would not be among them. His eyes opened. Unless she was returning his own daughter to him. If Zoe was with her, that would be different.

He finally slept, a fitful kind of sleep, filled with dreams of lost girls and burning vehicles.

* * *

Sam woke at six o'clock. He always did. He got up and showered, trying not to wake Sophie. If it had been any normal day, he would have gone out for a run before showering, but things being what they were, he decided against it. Standing beneath the torrent of hot water, he started to rehearse what he was going to say to Sophie about the change of plan. Mike's idea about a late-night call from Greece did sound pretty convincing, and he hoped a ten-year-old would swallow it without too many questions. She seemed to have accepted all the crap the foster parents had fed to her. They certainly controlled the kids, but he wondered who controlled *them*. And what on earth could be behind this apparently benevolent set-up? Taking in orphaned children and keeping them safe. Safe from what?

He turned the shower to cold and gasped, the freezing water blotting out the frightening thoughts that had suddenly come into his mind.

He dried himself and got dressed, pondering the warning that had been sent to Mike. It had been swift and devastating. Okay, his brother had enough money to simply buy another car while he waited for the insurance to be sorted out, but none of this had been meant as an inconvenience — it was meant to scare him, and it had done that with knobs on!

Sam considered exactly what had happened and came to the conclusion that although Julia might well be capable of sending a threatening note, causing a conflagration in a car park didn't sound like the way she operated at all. She knew Mike well, and that he was basically a hard-working, honest man, good at his job. Maybe that was the problem — his job. Technologically speaking, Julia knew very well what Mike was capable of. Perhaps she had decided to stop him in his tracks, before he could start meddling and do her and her campaign, whatever that was, any serious damage.

Sam went to the kitchen and filled the kettle. The thing was, if it wasn't Julia and whoever she was working with who had torched Mike's car, it meant that the nameless, faceless people who were a danger to Sophie were right here in town, and very much aware of what he and Mike were planning. Now that thought really did scare him.

He made himself a cup of tea and decided that if it did turn out to be the latter, there was one alternative to locking themselves in and keeping a low profile. After all, if these people had tracked Mike, they had to know where he and the girl were holed up, didn't they? He could pack a few things, take Sophie, and drive like the clappers out of there. He knew a place they could go to where no one would find them, and thanks to his work in the police, he knew how to do it without attracting any followers. It all depended on whether Mike's warning had come from Julia, or from her opponents in the war for Sophie. He had been told she was priceless. He held this priceless child's fate in his hands.

Sam took a gulp of his hot tea and winced. Whatever he was embroiled in was deadly serious, and it looked like Mike had been right when he'd said that Sam was about to jeopardise his precious career. As far as he could make out, it was teetering on the edge already, and if he took off with a ten-year-old kid in tow, he could bid it *auf Wiedersehen*, for ever.

He sighed. Meanwhile, all he could think about were two innocent little girls, their lives controlled by some very bad people. Sophie and Zoe deserved better, and if Sam was their only available help, then so be it. He wasn't about to turn his back on either of them.

He got up and looked in the fridge. He had eggs, bacon, tomatoes, and some hash browns. He would cook them a really good breakfast, and tell Sophie that basically something was wrong, and they had to decide whether to stay or go. Of course, the ultimate decision was down to him, but he thought he'd give her a chance to have her say. He had a feeling she'd appreciate it, and he wanted to involve her as much as he dared. Her whole life had been controlled by others; she deserved to think for herself. She was a very bright child, and he reckoned she'd handle it.

Taking the various items from the fridge, he suddenly wondered about Mike. Should he tell his brother of his intentions, or leave him completely out of it? Maybe they should just go, telling no one. It would be safer for Mike.

Lifting his skillet from the drawer under the hob, he thought again. Or would it be safer? It could be worse. Suppose they got hold of Mike and tried to make him tell them where Sam and the kid had gone, and Mike didn't know? Just how desperate were these people? Well, he knew the answer to that one all right. So, he would tell Mike, suggesting he take an impromptu holiday, accidentally forgetting to give his staff the destination.

He set out strips of bacon under the grill, already feeling better for having a back-up plan in place. Sam knew it was rather early to wake the child, but this could be an important day and they needed to hit the ground running. He'd have his discussion with Sophie, after which he'd make the big decision — to either batten down the hatches or do a disappearing act.

* * *

DI Terri Lander was in very early. There had been a development in a case she was running and she needed to grab the overnight intel before the troops arrived. If everything went according to plan, she might have an arrest before lunchtime.

She stared at the report she had just removed from the printer and smiled grimly. Yep, looking good! In some excitement, Terri formulated an action plan, ran over it twice, and then chose the perfect team for the hit. She wrote their names on a memo pad, suddenly sad that one was missing.

For the first time since he'd gone on leave, she felt anxious about Sam. Certainly she missed his presence as her right-hand man — he was the sounding board for her ideas — but this was different, and she wasn't sure why. Maybe she was worrying about how he was faring with his young daughter, who would no doubt keep talking about her mother, the ex-wife that he would prefer to forget. Still, it was odd.

With a grunt, she dragged her mind back to the case in hand. Sam would have to come later, but as soon as this raid was over and the cell doors had clanged shut, she would ring him and ask if she could meet up with him and Zoe.

When every last thing was in place and she felt happy about the timing, she cast a quick eye over the reports that had come in from the night before. It didn't hurt to be in the know about the minor things; there were often little events that turned out to be connected to their more serious investigations.

Nothing of importance there, she thought, and was just about to close them down when she saw a name underneath a report about a car that had caught fire in an office block car park. The name was Mike Helsdown.

Terri frowned. Sam's brother Mike's car had not merely caught fire, it had apparently been torched — the crew who had attended suspected arson. Her frown deepened. Mike? Surely not. She'd met him several times and he was definitely not the sort to attract trouble.

With an effort, Terri set the report aside, and pulled on her DI's hat once more. She was about to command a serious drugs raid and must focus on that. But the report had strengthened her resolve to contact Sam as soon as it was over.

* * *

Sam shouldn't have worried about waking Sophie early. She had smelled the breakfast cooking and was up before he called her.

'That smells very different from the Greek breakfasts we had on the island,' she murmured, apparently a little unsure of what she was about to eat. 'We have lovely breads and pastries, and fruit and yoghurt — all high in nutritional value and good for us. Is this good too?'

'In its way, sunshine, it's the best, especially if you have a big day ahead.' A slight exaggeration, but it *was* good, in a different way.

'Did I hear the telephone ring really late last night, Daddy?'

Thanks, thought Sam, *the perfect way in.* 'Yes, you did, sweetheart, and I need to talk to you about something really important, okay?'

She nodded seriously. 'Was it Julia?'

Even better! 'I think so, but I can't be sure.' He set down a plate in front of her and began his prepared speech.

Sophie listened intently, and her face darkened. 'I hope everyone's okay. I'd hate for something bad to happen to Florence and Jim. They must be missing me a bit, like they did Costas, although that was different, wasn't it? He was gone for ever. I've gone to where I was meant to be, with my father.'

His heart lurched. How long could he keep lying to this lovely little girl? 'I'm sure Jim and Florence will be fine, honey. It sounds like it's you and I who have to worry. Until I hear more, we need to lie low. I've no idea what this "situation" is that Julia, or whoever that was who rang me, was talking about, but she sounded very concerned about our safety.' He looked at her intently. 'Sophie, did you ever have cause to believe that you or the other children were being . . .

how can I put it? Well, protected? Did you ever feel like you were treated very differently to other children?'

'Oh yes,' she said, crunching on the crispy bacon and clearly enjoying it. 'Especially when Costas was alive. He used to have all sorts of ideas about us being very special, and not like normal kids. We didn't quite believe him, because he did have some stupid ideas too, but I often wondered if the kids we saw playing up in the hills in the olive groves had rules like we did. They seemed to be able to go anywhere, do anything, not like us.'

Sam took a chance. 'I'm going to be honest with you, Sophie, and talk to you like an adult, because you're not a silly child, and I believed what you said about not liking lies. I think Costas was right. You *are* special. I also think you have been protected very carefully with some important plan in place for your future, and something has gone wrong.'

She looked up at him. 'Thank you for being honest, but now I'm a bit afraid. Is someone bad looking for me?'

'I don't know, kid, but they'll have to get past me, and that could take some doing, I promise.' *At least that's the truth,* Sam thought grimly. 'But we need to make a plan, you and I together, okay? We'll sort this and make everything right again.'

'What did she actually tell you, Dad?'

'Only that there was a problem, and we should be very careful until they have sorted it out. I took that to mean stay at home here until we hear from them again. It's that, or we pack some things and go play hide and seek.'

'Like, go on the run? I read a book about two children who did that when they tried to save their parents from being wrongly imprisoned. It was American, and a bit scary.' Sophie's eyes were wide. 'I'm not sure I'm brave enough for that.'

'I'm surprised that your foster parents let you read a book about that sort of thing,' said Sam with a grin.

'They didn't. Costas used to sneak out sometimes, and he brought me books. I think he might have stolen it from a tourist. He told us about a hotel not far down the coast. He found a way to get in and would sometimes bring back things that the people who stayed there left lying around by the pool. Darius would have been furious if he found out, but that was Costas, he was a daredevil.' Sophie looked sad whenever she mentioned him, and Sam came to the conclusion that they'd been closer than she had admitted.

'Well, if we did go away, it would be nothing like your book, I promise. There is a place I know that would be great for a few days' holiday. No one would know we were there. Julia, or whoever, could still contact us by phone, so we wouldn't be out of touch. Then, when their problem is all solved, we can come back and start again.'

'Where is it?' she asked tentatively.

'Best I don't tell you, honey. But it'll take about an hour by car, no longer. And I think you'd like it.'

'I hope it's warm, wherever it is — I'm feeling a bit cold over here.'

He considered the clothes that she had been sent over with and decided that even if they did decide to go, they'd have to wait for the Amazon delivery to arrive. He got to his feet and turned the heating up a couple of degrees. Then he went to where she was sitting and gave her a hug. 'Don't be frightened, Sophie. I won't let anything bad happen to you.'

They continued eating their breakfast. After a while, Sophie said, 'How come I'm special?'

'You have a remarkable grasp of mathematics for a girl of ten, you know. You can add up a whole shopping trolley full of stuff to the penny — that's way ahead of most folk. And you're still young: who knows just how clever you might become when you're older!' Sam smiled at her. 'That makes you pretty special, and that's only what I know of you. What else can you do?'

The child looked unsure of herself. 'It's just numbers. I see numbers . . .' She looked confused. 'I'm not s'posed to talk about it, Daddy. Not to anyone.'

Disappointed, he said, 'Hey, that's all right, honestly. But I know you are great at figures, so it can't hurt, can it, if I just ask if you can do mental arithmetic.'

She gave a little shrug. 'Of course I can.'

He took out his mobile phone and pressed the key for the calculator. 'Okay, Einstein, what's six times ninety-two?'

'Five hundred and fifty-two. But that's kid's stuff. Can we leave it there?'

'One more?' He grinned hopefully. 'Go on! I think you're amazing.'

She rolled her eyes. 'Okay, just one more, but make it better than the last one.'

'One hundred and twenty-seven, multiplied by seventy-four.'

Two blinks, then, 'Nine thousand, three hundred and ninety-eight. Can I have a glass of orange juice, please?'

He stared at his calculator. She had been so fast that it had taken him longer to key in the numbers, let alone retrieve the answer. He stood up and went to the fridge. Mike had asked if she was a genius. Sam still didn't know the answer to that, but she certainly had a pretty awesome talent. He placed the glass in front of her. 'Okay, back to the matter in hand. Do we stay or do we go?'

'I'll do whatever you think is safest,' she said with gravity. 'You're a policeman, Daddy, you'll always do the right thing.'

How he wished that were true! 'Right, then, we'll wait until your new clothes arrive. Amazon usually delivers before midday, so I'll have plenty of time to decide. Meanwhile, suppose you have a shower and get dressed while I clear the dishes.' He took her plate. 'So, what did you think of the Helsdown full English breakfast?'

'I could get to like it, Daddy, but not every day, thank you. I don't think it's really all that healthy, do you?' She gave him an old-fashioned look.

'Relax, Sophie, it was a treat, just once in a while.' He didn't miss the relief on her face, but he also noted that she'd cleared every morsel from her plate. Okay, she wasn't his daughter, but he really liked this kid.

* * *

By eleven thirty Sophie had a new wardrobe. She was now clad in warm fleece-lined joggers, a long-sleeved T-shirt and zip-up teddy jacket. She had already sorted out a small selection of her favourite new clothes, underwear and pyjamas, folded them carefully and put them into one of Sam's sports holdalls. She put her 'essentials' — things a ten-year-old cannot possibly do without — into a neat floral backpack that he had thoughtfully added to the very large order. She had calmly advised Sam that if they stayed, that was fine, but she didn't want to have to pack in a hurry, so better she did it now and not forget anything.

Sam had done the same, only he merely threw in a few items of outside wear. He spent a lot more time on his particular 'essentials' — phone charger, money, credit cards, a laptop, paracetamol, a first aid kit and a small basic survival kit that he always put in the car if he was taking a few days out hiking, a Swiss knife and, lastly, a fourth-generation Glock 17 semi-automatic pistol and a box of ammunition. This he very carefully concealed at the bottom of his bag, well away from Sophie's eyes. Julia had said to protect the child with his life, and since Zoe's safety also depended on it, he fully intended to do just that.

He had never pointed a gun at another living being in his life. It went against everything he believed in, but he had won trophies in competition shooting, and had a very good eye. If someone threatened Sophie, Sam was pretty sure he could break the habit of a lifetime. He still couldn't kill, but a well-aimed shot could certainly be a game-changer. He prayed it wouldn't come to that, but at least he was prepared.

He did a final check, already knowing that they couldn't stay here. The very radical warning his brother had received told him it was too risky.

He went back into the lounge and found Sophie working on her tablet. He had handed her the TV remote control, but she had chosen to do her homework instead. A quick glance revealed lists of figures, which she rather distractedly declared to be a Fibonacci sequence. He walked away, shaking his head.

He roamed around his flat making sure that nothing was left switched on, and that he'd taken all perishable food out of the fridge. This was all packed in a cool box, along with other edibles and drinks, to take with them. To save time, he took it out to his car and put it in the boot. He was careful to lock the car again, recalling the fate of Mike's Toyota.

As he went back into the lounge, he heard Sophie say, 'Oh-oh! That's not supposed to happen.'

Mike went across to look and saw that the screen was blank. He was about to check the battery when three words in white flashed onto the black screen. *Vges exo! Tora!*

He saw Sophie's mouth drop open, then saw he had a message on his phone. *Get out! Now!*

'What does that mean?' He pointed urgently to Sophie's tablet.

'It's Greek. It says, "Get out! Now!"'

'Hurry, Sophie, get your things.' He ran into his room and gathered up his bags.

In less than five minutes, they were in the car. Just as he began to drive away, Sophie called out, 'Stop! Look! It's Uncle Mike getting out of that taxi.'

He cursed silently. He saw his brother throw some money at the driver and, grabbing a small leather tote bag, hurry towards them. Then he saw Mike's face. It was almost white with fear. Sam threw open his door. 'What on earth . . . ?'

'Look at this, Sam! Pushed through my letter box.' His hand shaking, he passed Sam a sheet of paper.

Get out now, or you could see a far more dangerous rerun of last night!

Sam didn't hesitate. 'Get in the back, quick! That vacation I mentioned? Well, you're on it.'

CHAPTER FIVE

'Where are we going?' asked Mike.

Sam chose not to tell him. 'Somewhere I go to chill out when I get bogged down in a tough investigation. It helps me get my head together.'

'I never knew about it,' murmured Mike. 'You never said, did you?'

'I've never told anyone. And it's quite safe. I share it with a mate in the force, and it's in his name, so no one can trace us that way.' Thank goodness he hadn't argued the point with his friend when they'd rented it. 'He's on secondment to another force right now and up to his neck, so he won't be back. It's probably the best place we can go right now.'

He drove fast, but carefully, as he couldn't afford to either be stopped for speeding or have an accident. He kept his eye on the rear-view mirror.

After two miles he spotted the powerful Audi some two or three cars behind him. He couldn't be certain, but the alarm bells were ringing. He made a couple of slight detours off the main road, then picked it up again a few miles on. The Audi reappeared. Sam gritted his teeth, grateful for having chosen this particular model of car. The Audi had power and speed, but he could go off-road if necessary, and his had far better manoeuvrability.

'Okay, guys, hang on tight. We have company and I have no wish to share this journey with anyone else.' Sophie gasped, so he patted her knee. 'It's all right, sweetheart, you're good at maths, this is what I'm good at.'

She smiled at him. 'Right, Daddy. Let's go.'

It took him five minutes to lose the Audi, but a few seconds later he realised he'd picked up a motorcycle, its rider wearing black leathers and a black helmet and visor. This was a different ballgame altogether, and took a bit of thought. There was one chance, and it might not work, but the weather was in his favour and it was worth a try. 'We're taking to the fen lanes now. I know this route well, so just trust me.' He accelerated forward.

Mike leaned forward and gave Sophie's shoulder a squeeze. 'Don't worry, Soph, it's fine. We're in good hands, so long as you like white-knuckle rides.'

The black-garbed rider stuck with him, but Sam was gambling on the fact that he knew the narrow fen lanes better than the motorcyclist. It was a bad route for any vehicle to attempt, unless you were driving one of the massive tractors that used it regularly, churning up verges into deep, water-filled muddy furrows and reducing the poorly tarmacked surface to a minefield of cracks and potholes.

Sam had seen that it was an enduro bike, capable of handling difficult terrain, but even so, the lane he had picked was a bastard to negotiate, more so if you didn't know it. His lips set in a grim smile. It wasn't the lane that would catch out the motorbike, it was the little detour he was planning — it had a sting in its tail. 'Thank heavens for bad weather,' he muttered as he saw his objective ahead.

In the middle of miles of open farmland sat Hazelden House. The rambling old building, once grand, had lost its splendour. It now functioned as a farm, a stable, and a small rescue centre for ill-treated or abandoned animals. If you entered by the long shrub-lined drive off this lane, you could pass in front of the house itself, and out again much further down the lane.

Sam swung the wheel in a vicious sharp turn. 'Grit your teeth, you two!' he shouted, and they hit the cattle grid hard, jolting Mike and Sophie. They gasped, but he was across it in moments.

Not so the bike.

In the mirror, Sam watched the rear wheel hit the wet metal grid and do a rather spectacular skid before catapulting bike and rider high into the air and flipping over.

By the time they were back on the lane, they were alone. In another ten minutes, and after several further deviations, Sam was fairly sure they had lost their escorts. He took a road in the opposite direction to his hideaway, and slowly, and by a very circuitous route indeed, brought them closer. By the time he was on the final leg of the journey, he knew for sure that they were no longer being tailed, and he relaxed.

'Game over, folks, we win.'

We made it this time, he thought to himself. *But what next?*

* * *

Saltire Lakes was a little-known oasis of peace. Hidden away down a leafy lane, it nestled between the grounds of an old abbey and a maze of winding lanes that led out over acres of arable fields. All but invisible from the road, it consisted of six log cabins above two small lakes. The lakes —really little more than large ponds — were the remains of old salterns, or salt works, hundreds of which dotted the county, dating back to the fifteenth and sixteenth centuries, some even as far back as Roman times. None of the cabins were lived in permanently; the owners rented them on a yearly basis. Nearly all the people who used them, for short breaks, long holidays, or just a day here and there, renewed their leases every January. Sam and his friend had kept theirs for over five years, and Sam found it the perfect escape from the stresses of difficult investigations.

Following the familiar track beside the abbey, he felt they'd been granted a reprieve. At least, while they were here, they wouldn't be threatened.

Sam's phone rang. He saw the name DI Terri Lander and refused the call. *Not now, Terri!* He had a feeling she might text him, however, and before they had even arrived at his cabin, he received a voicemail message from her.

'Where the hell are you, Helsdown? I've been to your house, and unless you lost your key and decided to jemmy your front door open, you've had visitors! Ring me!' There was a short pause, then she added, 'Please, Sam. Just ring.'

He knew he must, but he'd get the others inside first, and get the wood burner going.

'Looks like we got away not a moment too soon,' said Mike grimly, as Sam dragged their bags out of the car. 'I just hope they didn't trash your home.'

'Me too. I hope they were only looking for us, not my treasured possessions, or Sophie's new lurex socks.' He looked at the little girl, who was wandering around outside. 'She doesn't seem to have been too bothered by what Terri said, so let's play it down while we're all together, okay?'

Mike agreed. Sam unlocked the cabin and ushered them inside.

'This is great!' exclaimed Sophie.

'You're a dark horse.' Mike elbowed him. 'Didn't even want to share it with your brother. You selfish sod!' He clapped his hand over his mouth. 'Sorry, Soph! But I mean to say, really!'

Sophie giggled. 'It's lovely! I'm sure I'd be very happy living here.'

The cedarwood cabin had two bedrooms, a small modern kitchen, a shower room and toilet, and an open-plan lounge. He and Ryan had added some powerful plug-in ceramic panel heaters, and with the log burner going, it would be warm and cosy in no time. Sam fetched the food from the car and asked Mike to put it away for him while he lit the fire. He was glad he had left the fridge freezer plugged in, and he knew there were several ready meals, bread, and chips in the freezer. At least they wouldn't starve.

Wondering that the hell he was going to say to Terri, Sam climbed back in the car and made the call, opting to tell her as near the truth as he dared.

'I'm with my daughter, Terri. We decided on a couple of days somewhere quiet to get to know each other all over again. Now you say I've had a break-in. So, what happened? Any damage?'

Terri sounded relieved to hear from him. 'I had an interview to do not far from your flat, so I called by, mainly to say hello to Zoe, and see how you were doing. I was going to suggest we all go out for a pizza one evening. I thought I'd leave you a note if you were out. The outer door was fine, but then I saw your front door. It was well jemmied, Sam, and none too delicately either.'

'Shit!' said Sam. 'And I can't get back just yet either. Did they take much that you could see?'

'It's odd, actually.' Terri sounded puzzled. 'There wasn't any real damage. To be honest, I'd have said that they were looking for something. Drawers searched, cupboards open, but no crap anywhere, no graffiti, no wanton destruction.' She gave a little grunt. 'Yeah, they were after something specific, Sam. Any ideas?'

He played it cool. 'I don't get it. I've got nothing that would be important to anyone.'

'Your kid's room seemed to be the focus of the search, that was well turned over. I have to tell you, Sam, I don't like it. Especially not on top of your brother having his car burnt out.'

He swallowed hard. So, she knew about that too. 'Surely that had to be a couple of little scrotes out for a bit of vandalism.' It sounded lame even to him. 'It can't be connected to my flat.'

'Hello? Is Detective Sergeant Helsdown around, please? Because I seem to be speaking to a moron. Since when have you believed in coincidence?' She sounded both gruff and anxious. 'Okay, Sam, how about you tell me what's going on.'

Sam drew in a shaky breath. 'I'm in trouble, Terri. But please, please, don't ask me about it. One, I *cannot* tell you. Two, I *will* not tell you, because I know damn well my job is on the line here, and with that shite of a superintendent gunning for you, I'm not having him shafting you for shit that's going on in my life.'

For a moment she said nothing, then very softly, 'I'm your friend, Sam. If you're in trouble, I'll help you, sod Roger Clarke. Sod all gold braid, actually. I don't even think I want to stay if you're going to give up the ghost and not fight back. Let me help.'

He wanted nothing more than her help, but he dared not involve her. 'Terri, I would. I swear there is no one else I'd turn to, but even I don't know what is going on. I just know we are in trouble, and in danger. If I tell you one thing, it might help you understand. If I make one wrong move, my daughter's safety, maybe her life, is threatened. Please see that I have no choice.'

'Can you tell me where you are?'

'No.'

'Have you got a pen handy?'

He rooted in the glove box. 'Yes, why?'

'I'm going to give you a mobile number. It's direct to me. Even the station doesn't have this one. No one has it.'

She rattled off a number. 'I'll put it straight into my phone.'

'Under something innocuous, like Auntie Gladys, or "gas engineer." Just remember, I'm here if you need me, twenty-four seven, and I mean that.'

He breathed a sigh of relief that she wasn't pressing him. 'Terri, can you get someone to make the flat secure for me? I'll settle up when this is over.'

'Already organised. I've asked Handy Andy to do a bit of a repair job on the woodwork on the quiet-like, and a locksmith is going to replace the damaged lock later this afternoon. I'll keep the new key for you, for when you come back.'

Andy Fairbrother was a retired copper making a living as an odd-job man; he was a very good one too, and discreet. Terri had chosen the right bloke. 'I really appreciate that, but I have to get back inside now. Even though I think we are safe, I—'

'Shut up, will you?'

In the background, he could hear a shout going out on the car radio. It sounded urgent.

He heard Terri say, 'Give me that address again, Officer! Ah, fucking hell! On my way!'

He felt a shiver of apprehension. Her next words told him he was right to worry.

'Your brother's house, Sam. Is it called Japonica Lodge, in Burley Avenue?'

His mouth went dry. 'Another break-in?'

'No, Sam, but it sounds like his car isn't his only possession to have attracted that arsonist. The house went up like a fireball a few minutes ago. Oh, Sam, I just pray to God that Mike wasn't inside!'

'It's okay, Terri. He's here, he's with me, and he's safe — at least I hope he is.'

'Thank heavens. But, Sam, what the hell have you got yourself mixed up in?'

'I wish I knew, Terri.'

'Well, if it wasn't bad enough before, mate, you do realise that now you'll have us lot pulling out all the stops to find you? This is serious shit.' She went silent for a few moments. 'Listen, I'll try to steer them away from you, I'll say the three of you are on holiday, I'd heard from you just before all this crap hit the fan but I've no idea where you are, just that the signal's rubbish. I don't know how long I can hold them up, so you'd better get your finger out and try to do something from your end. And keep in touch on that private number. I've got to go. Please, please take care, and guard that little girl with your life.'

The phone went dead. *Guard that little girl with your life.* Julia's words exactly. Though Terri had no idea that the child she was referring to wasn't Zoe but an entirely different girl.

* * *

Terri stood behind the barrier and watched the fire crews working feverishly to get the worst of the blaze under control. She was filled with rage. How could anyone deliberately burn down someone else's home, along with all their treasured belongings, their cherished memories? It was like stealing a massive part of someone's life, with no chance of ever getting it back. Of all the deliberate acts of criminal destruction, Terri hated fire the most. Why consign to the flames the things a person loved most — a photograph, a letter, a token from a wedding cake. A child's first bootee. No insurance in the world was able to recompense the victim for what they had invested in their home.

Fortunately for the neighbours, Mike's house was detached, set well back, and some way from the others. She saw a white-faced family clustered together in the road, staring in horror as the house next door fast became a blackened and charred ruin. At least they had been spared.

The fire chief came over and stood beside her. 'Definitely arson, DI Lander, no doubt about it. We've contained an area close to the front door and it clearly shows the fire started there. I'd say that accelerant tipped through the letterbox got it going, but we suspect someone broke in earlier and spread other flammable material around the house to make sure the whole place went up. Someone wanted this place gutted, and they weren't leaving anything to chance.'

Having ensured that everything possible was being done, Terri returned to her car. She sat staring at the conflagration, trying to work it all out. Sam had said he was in trouble, but this was trouble of the monumental kind.

At work, Terri was renowned for her analytical brain. Given a puzzle she could work it out like a mathematical problem, working from proven fact, adding known probables like laying bricks on top of one another, and sifting through the possibilities to see what fitted and what could be discarded. But where Sam Helsdown was concerned, her attempts at reasoning left her none the wiser. It wasn't just this particular mess, it was the last one too. That terrible case so badly handled by MIT, from which he'd emerged with a cloud hanging over his whole position in the force, that had cast his loyalty to the force and his colleagues in doubt, and could have labelled him a rogue cop. She had never believed this to be the case, and she was eventually proved right, but mud sticks. Sam's one and only secondment into a major crime unit had marked him as untrustworthy in everyone's eyes except hers.

If anyone but Terri had been his DI at the time, he'd have been history, and the force would have lost a good and very brave detective. She had probably saved his career, but in the process, he had lost his wife. The person meddling in places she oughtn't to have been, talking to people she shouldn't and generally acting very much outside the law had not been Sam, but his MIT partner and ex-wife, Julia Berkman.

Terri thought back to that awful time and sighed. Nothing had ever been proven against Julia, and although she had left the force, she had done so voluntarily. Sam had been left to pick up the pieces of a shattered career, come to terms with a divorce, and try to get access to his daughter. Julia had moved away and Sam had been less and less able to see little Zoe. He had been close to his daughter and he swore that one day he'd have her back permanently. Terri wasn't sure what had happened, exactly, but suddenly Julia was working abroad and had taken Zoe with her. Sam's pleas and demands were all eclipsed by whatever important work Julia was doing, the months became a year, and so it went. Until today.

Terri sat, staring at nothing. Sam's troubles must have started when he received a message from Julia saying his daughter was coming for a holiday, which meant the trouble he was in was connected to, or caused by, Julia. Again!

Well, she wasn't going to work this out without more information to go on. There were far too many questions, one being: why target Mike in such a devastating fashion? Was it a case of hit the nearest and dearest? Or did Mike know something about what was going on? Or — and this made her really wonder — was it to do with the fact that Mike owned a big IT company and was brilliant at using the technology? It was very possible that they were removing the one man who could be Sam's ace card in this game. Perhaps 'they', whoever they were, were trying to isolate Sam and Zoe. Why they should do something like that gave rise to some very scary hypotheses.

One of these possibilities — that this was a plan hatched by Julia — would mean that Mike himself was still under serious threat. Terri didn't hate anyone, except the superintendent, but she disliked Julia Berkman intensely. She certainly hated what she had done to Sam. This theory saw Julia manipulating Sam into running away with Zoe, leaving the way open for her to accuse him of abducting her. Sam had always been putty in her hands; he would probably never dream that this whole thing had been concocted to ensure he never saw his daughter again.

Terri turned the engine on. She was wasting time sitting here hypothesising. She had work to do, and she needed to be back at base to do it. She had to try and find a way to keep the police from hunting for Mike and Sam. They needed all the time she could give them to keep themselves safe and find out what the hell was going on.

CHAPTER SIX

This was one of the hardest things he would ever have to do. His heart ached for his brother. He had lost the home he had loved, and according to the text Sam had received from Terri Lander, everything in it. To add to the problem of how to impart such terrible news, he couldn't do it in front of Sophie for fear of frightening her even more.

He pretended they needed to make sure they had enough wood to see them through their stay. Once he and Mike were outside, he realised that there was going to be no easy way to tell him, so he blurted it out.

Mike didn't speak for a while, but the hurt, the *anguish* on his face, spoke for him. All he could say was, 'Why? Why me?'

'Tell me the truth, Mike,' said Sam gently. 'Were you still trying to chase down Julia?'

Mike nodded bleakly. 'But not after you warned me about Zoe being threatened. The thing is, I failed to lift a tracker I've been running ever since she took Zoe away from you.'

Sam felt stunned. 'You've been following her movements all along?'

'From the moment her plane took off.'

‘But why? Back then she was just working abroad. Why keep tabs on her then? I was hearing from her occasionally anyway.’ Sam’s head was a mess. ‘And she’d been cleared of all involvement in that bad case when she was in MIT. I don’t get it.’

‘Because you never ever saw the bigger picture, brother! I always knew that bitch hadn’t finished with you. There is so much more to all this, and somehow, I swear it hinges around Zoe. Now this horrible charade with that poor damned kid in there! Who is she, Sam? Who are we on the run with?’ He raised his voice, furious now. ‘You don’t know! I don’t know! Even the kid doesn’t know. But someone does. *Julia* knows, all right.’ He spat the name out.

Sam felt as if he been decked by a prize fighter. All this time his brother had been trying to look out for him. Zoe too. And it appeared to have cost him dearly. ‘Jesus, what a mess,’ he whispered. ‘Oh, Mike, I’m so sorry for what has happened.’

Mike was silent, either boiling with rage or calming down, Sam wasn’t sure.

When he finally spoke, he said, ‘We can’t leave Sophie for too long, Sam. When she’s gone to sleep, we’ll talk, and as you said, there’ll be no more lies. But you really need to listen to me, because this is far from over.’

‘Yeah, it seems I do,’ Sam said quietly. ‘Maybe I should have done so from the beginning.’

They filled a basket with logs and carried it back to the cabin. They would have to act cheerful in front of Sophie. It wasn’t going to be easy.

Surprisingly, Mike turned out to be a brilliant actor. He stepped inside wearing a broad smile. ‘All stocked and ready to go, Soph, you won’t get cold in here. Hey, are they jigsaws on that shelf, Sam? Maybe Sophie would like to give one a go? I’ll help, I used to love ’em when I was a kid.’

Feeling like howling in pain and sorrow, Sam did his best to follow suit. ‘Sure. Ryan had his nephews down here back in the summer, teaching them to fish. They left quite a few games and puzzles here. Help yourself.’

The day dragged on while they acted the parts of jolly father and uncle. Luckily, Sophie was soon tired after their abrupt exodus from the flat, the car chase, and finding herself in a completely different place. She asked to go to bed not long after they'd eaten.

He had given her the room with the double bed, leaving the second, which had two singles, for him and Mike. At least they all had proper beds, and if Sam and his brother needed to talk, they could do so out of the girl's hearing. He left the heater on in her room, so it was pleasantly warm, and he suspected she would fall asleep quickly.

'We haven't heard from Julia,' she said, when he went in to say goodnight.

'No,' he said, biting back a less than charitable response. 'So I'm guessing she hasn't yet sorted everything out in Greece. I'm sure she'll contact us soon, and then we can go home again, sweetheart. You get to sleep now, and if you're worried about anything, you just call, okay? We're only next door.'

'It's nice here, Daddy. I hope we can stay for a little while at least. Night night. Love you.'

He swallowed hard. Each time she called him Daddy, he wanted to howl. He silently cursed Julia for what was happening. 'Night, kiddo. Love you too.'

Back in the lounge, Mike was sitting on the sofa, legs outstretched, having poured them each a drink.

Sam flopped down next to him. 'What did you manage to bring with you?' He pointed to Mike's brown leather grab-bag, still zipped up.

Mike pulled a face. 'Razor, toothbrush, underwear, socks, medication, charger, a laptop, money, credit cards, and my lucky Smurf.'

'No clothes?'

'Nope. Strangely, when I read that note, I decided not to hang around going through my wardrobe.' He looked fierce. 'Not that I have one anymore.' He took a slug of his scotch.

'But you did remember your lucky Smurf.' Sam couldn't hide his smile. Mike had had the little blue cartoon character toy since his childhood and swore it brought him luck.

Sam was thinking it might be losing its powers when Mike said, 'And since I was out of the house when Guy Fawkes came a-calling, I can verify that it still works.'

While he realised that the reality of what had happened had probably not sunk in yet, Sam marvelled at his brother's capacity to accept misfortune. He recalled a time when they were boys and some local louts had damaged Mike's precious bike. Sam would have been incandescent, but Mike had just shrugged and said, 'Oh well, I suppose they took it out on a bike, rather than another little kid.' Then, even though their father would have paid for a replacement, he had worked at odd jobs to buy himself a new one, reckoning it was his fault for leaving it outside the paper shop.

'You're incredible, you really are,' said Sam sincerely. 'Now, I think we should talk about where we go from here.'

Mike rubbed hard at his chin. 'And like it or not, I'm going to tell you how I feel about it all. It won't be an easy job convincing me otherwise, I warn you.'

Sam took a breath. 'First off, can I ask what was your real reason for tracking Julia?'

'Mainly because I didn't take kindly to what she did to my brother, like wrecking his life and almost costing him his beloved career. Oh, and I wasn't too keen on her marrying you, dumping you, and buggering off with your daughter either.' Mike looked at his brother over the rim of his glass. 'I don't trust her. I never have, from the moment I met her. There was some dirty business going on back in your MIT days, and Julia was mixed up in it. She used you, and she used me too. I know you loved her, but I truly don't think she's the woman you believed her to be. And please don't give me the old "But you didn't know her the way I did" shit. Well. There it is.'

Sam had been about to utter those very words but saw the sense in refraining. Instead, he said, 'How did she take advantage of you?'

'She used our expertise, I'm not too sure what for. She was a fixture in my office for a while, having us access all manner of sensitive information, but, as you well know, she had the clearance, so how could we refuse?' He shrugged. 'I'm just not sure if she passed it all to the right people.'

'Oh, Mike. If we weren't sitting here dreading what will happen next, I'd have said that you were wrong, that she was always a damned good police officer. After all, I worked right alongside her, in uniform and as a detective, and until now I thought all she was guilty of was trying too hard to get the bastards that we were going after.' He shook his head. 'I really never believed she could be turned, never. Now I don't know what to think. And what's driving me mad is why make me pass off this lovely child as my daughter? Why make me the protector of something so precious? She said Sophie is priceless, and I do believe that.' He stared at Mike. 'Even though I have doubts about a whole lot of things, I do know that she would never put Zoe in jeopardy. She loves our child, and I *have* to believe that she loved me too, once. I could never have survived it all without that belief.' He grimaced. 'Yeah, I know, there were plenty of unanswered questions, about her going away for one, and there are far more now, but . . .' He spread out his hands. 'All I can say is that I am listening to you now, and I'm admitting to having doubts. Maybe I'm wrong about Julia. Maybe I always have been, but for Zoe's sake, I have to believe she's still loved. It's tearing me apart, and I'm out of my depth.'

His brother smiled at him affectionately. 'There are days when I'd like to rip those rose-tinted spectacles off your eyes and stamp on them, but it won't help anything right now. Let's try to work out what could possibly be driving her, or persons unknown, to be so brutal. My home is gone, Sam. My car is gone. The only thing left is my life. Are they wanting that too?'

Sam frowned, back in copper mode. 'You left one thing out. Your business. What if you know something you shouldn't? You know, through your work, or those trackers and traces you were using on Julia. What if you have some information that they, whoever they are, are afraid of, or want to suppress? Maybe they want to put the frighteners on you and make sure you don't use your computers.'

Mike said nothing for a while. Then, 'In that case why not torch the offices?'

'And kill a whole load of innocents — Samaritans and health workers? For a start, it would give rise to a worldwide media frenzy and draw massive attention to them. Totally counter-productive.' He paused. 'By the way, where did you trace Julia to?'

'In and out of at least three countries,' said Mike. 'Oh, and I wasn't going to tell you this, but she's here in the UK. She left Greece two days ago.'

Sam leaned forward. 'Alone?'

'Sorry, mate, but yes, alone. To Edinburgh.'

'Scotland?' It was no use asking why. Mike might be dogging her footsteps, but he would hardly have access to her thoughts.

'Yes, but sadly, I've been a bit too otherwise engaged of late to find out whether she's moved on.' He softened. 'Look, I'm not sure if this is helpful, but the last time she travelled with Zoe was two weeks ago, and as far as I can make out Zoe hasn't gone anywhere since.' He paused. 'Until I traced what I thought was her passport coming through Heathrow, on the flight Sophie was on. Oh, and I took a look at that passport of hers, it's one of the best fakes I've ever seen. I think your daughter is still where Julia left her last — in Holland.'

Holland? That was where Julia had worked when she left England, and where they had lived for a time. 'Julia has close friends in Leiden, which is just over half an hour southwest of Amsterdam, towards the coast. Maybe Zoe is with them.' He felt a tug at his heart. Perhaps the child was safe after all, and Julia was just making sure he did as she had demanded by pretending that Zoe was in danger. Would she really do that? He guessed it would depend on the seriousness of her request to keep Sophie safe. Mike would certainly believe that Julia was capable of deceiving him, and considering what had happened to him, he could be right.

They sat in silence for a while, drinking their whisky, then Sam said, 'I know you won't like this suggestion, and I'm only playing devil's advocate here, but had you considered that if it *was* Julia who sent you that note about getting out, she might have been protecting you? I mean, she could have said, "Wait at home where you will be contacted by phone," or something like that. Then you would have fried along with the house. It said to get out, so maybe it wasn't a threat at all, but she was alerting you to something that was about to happen — which it did.' He looked hard at his brother. 'I get the feeling that if they had wanted you dead, you would be by now.'

'Maybe you're right about the last bit, but I'm still not buying a kind-hearted Julia. Oh hell, Sam, if we could only discover who Sophie really is, we might have a chance of understanding what's behind it all.' He paused, narrowed his eyes. 'And are we really safe here?'

Sam didn't think they'd be safe anywhere until help came — if help ever did. 'Safer than anywhere else I can think of, but . . .' He drained his glass and immediately wanted another — not a good idea. He shouldn't have had the first one, really. If they had to move on in a hurry, he'd need to be firing on all cylinders. 'What are you thinking?'

'You have a signal out here, don't you?' Mike said.

He nodded. 'It's very good, actually. We even have Wi-Fi. Me and Ryan come here to relax, but we don't like to be completely out of touch—' He stopped. 'You want to keep searching, don't you?'

'I don't like being out of touch either.' Mike finished his drink and stared into the empty glass. 'I want to find out where I can obtain compensation and since I've nothing left to lose, I don't care how I get it.'

* * *

That night, after Mike had turned in, Sam went outside for a look at their surroundings. From his plot he could see two of the other cabins partly hidden among the trees around the lake. He was relieved to see that they were both in darkness and had no vehicles parked beside them. The other three were not visible from here; to see them you had to walk further along the lane that led to the second lake. He stood hesitating, unable to decide whether to take a look at them or stay close to the cabin and Sophie. He still felt fairly confident that no one knew they were here, but was afraid to stray far from his little ward. He decided to remain where he was. It was the middle of the week and winter; few people came at this time of year. Sometimes either he or Ryan had spent an entire week here and seen no one. He hoped it would be the same on this occasion — he could do without friendly neighbours calling by.

Sam's head was still full of Mike's revelations, but he had passed the point of trying to understand anything. Standing in the chilly night air, he decided to stop trying to fathom it all out — it was all speculation, anyway — and concentrate on keeping Sophie safe. He had to assume that what Julia had originally told him was true, and work from there. Narrowing his focus would help him to be his old sharp self again, not some dithering idiot who didn't know which way was up. In this way, he would also be protecting his own daughter. Eventually, help would come. If Julia really was back in the UK, as Mike believed, she could be organising their rescue right now.

The rain had stopped, and the night was damp and cold. From outside, the cabin looked cosy and inviting, and he could see why Sophie liked it. It had a kind of storybook feel to it — the little house in the woods, a million miles away from the flat monotonous fields of the Fens in which it really sat. It had been his refuge, returning him to sanity on more occasions than he could count, but he wondered if he would feel the same about it when this was over. It had been a very personal place, his own, he shared it with no one, except Ryan. Now, it felt like nothing more than a rental holiday cottage.

He turned back, scanning the path and the surrounding woods as he went, on the lookout for anything suspicious. Somehow he didn't feel particularly bothered. He had a distinct feeling that tonight all was well, and he would sleep soundly. God knows he needed it. Who knew what tomorrow would bring?

CHAPTER SEVEN

Terri had suffered through a night filled with frightening thoughts and nightmarish scenes. Finally, she fell into a fitful sleep at around three thirty, with the result that this morning she felt like shit.

Desperate to keep on top of the house fire business, last night she had made sure everyone knew that Mike Helsdown was away for a few days with his brother and his niece, who was visiting from abroad. She had taken it upon herself to act as contact between the police and either Mike or Sam, as soon as they came within range of a signal again. Since the station was busy with other cases, no one had argued with her.

Now, at seven thirty a.m. she was back behind her desk, armed with strong coffee and a Danish pastry. She'd informed the day shift that Mike could not be contacted, and that she was now asking around at places she knew Sam had frequented in the past. She added that she had checked with Mike's place of business, but he had left no indication as to where they were going. She hadn't, but no one with half a brain was going to be checking up on a DI.

Terri was using the time before her team arrived for work to do some investigating of her own. Her enquiries revolved entirely around Julia Berkman. She was doing what she always did and using known facts as her foundation stones.

Fact one: after almost two years of denying Sam access to Zoe, using all manner of weird and wonderful excuses, Julia had contacted Sam and informed him that she was sending his daughter to him for a holiday. Terri herself had sanctioned it, even though it had been at short notice.

Fact two: Sam had collected Zoe from the airport.

Fact three: Shortly after Zoe's arrival, Sam's brother Mike had his car torched.

Fact four: Sam and Zoe had disappeared from Sam's flat, which was immediately broken into and turned over.

Fact five: Mike's house had been destroyed by fire.

Final fact: Sam, Zoe and Mike were all together in an undisclosed location, and scared shitless.

Terri read through the list. It had all begun with Julia, so that was where she should start. The first thing she wanted to know was Julia's current whereabouts.

An hour passed. Search after search threw up no mention of Julia Berkman, other than the old sensational media reports with all the embellishments, including the rogue cop assumptions. These were followed much later by a handful of items in small print, saying she had been found innocent of all allegations.

Aware she was deviating from her research, Terri found herself trying to recall some of the names Sam had mentioned relating to the investigation that had gone so wrong. Its code name had been 'Operation Mitre'; everyone knew that, it had been on enough newspaper headlines. But what was the name of the man they had been investigating? Julia and Sam had been desperate to apprehend this person, and as soon as they got close, everything went wrong. The name had never been made public — in fact it never even made it out of the police files. Wentworth! That was it. Nicholas Wentworth. A rich businessman. More than merely rich, his wealth was excessive even for a top executive. It was believed at the time that he was involved in some heavyweight criminal activities, and Sam and Julia were certain that they were about to make connections that could bring him down.

Terri struggled to recall much more, since the whole thing had been buried very quickly following suggestions that the police team had acted 'inappropriately'. It had even been alleged that one of the officers was actually in the pay of the criminals. It had been messy, and quite horrible. Terri still didn't like to recall the emotional strain it had placed a whole division under. Absently, she typed in Wentworth's name. Immediately, a message appeared on her screen: '*Access Denied.*' It pulsated, accompanied by a beeping sound.

She deleted it, shocked that it was still considered too sensitive to be made available even to officers with a higher rank.

She glanced up. The CID office outside was filling up with staff, so she closed her computer down and went out to discuss their other cases. Sam's empty desk formed an enormous hollow in the middle of the busy room. If only he were sitting there, not running scared and beyond her help.

An hour and half later, assured that everything was running smoothly, Terri took herself off to get a coffee. Their station had lost its canteen due to cutbacks, but it did have a small café, which was a big improvement on the vending machines that had replaced most canteen facilities. She rarely went in there, usually sending someone down to pick up whatever she wanted, but today she went herself. She bought an americano, and instead of taking it back to her office to drink at her desk, she took it to a small table close to the door and sat down. Sam had crept back into her thoughts again, and she couldn't concentrate on anything else.

She was so deep in thought that she failed to notice the tall figure stop beside her table.

'I need a word, DI Lander.'

Her head snapped up. 'Oh, Chief Superintendent Ellwood. I'm so sorry, I was miles away.'

'So I see. Bring your drink up to my office, if you would.' He was already heading out into the corridor.

Terri hurried after him, half expecting to find the dread Roger Clarke already there, waiting to pounce on her for some infringement or other. It was bound to be a complaint. You didn't get called up in front of the chief without good reason.

She found they were alone and breathed a sigh of relief. Even so, she took her seat opposite his rather imposing desk feeling somewhat apprehensive. She liked Stefan Ellwood. He was a fair man, very imposing yet surprisingly thoughtful, and with a rather gentle manner beneath the dignified exterior. Years ago, she had worked with him when he was still a DI, and learned that in his case, what you saw was definitely not what you got. Stefan turned out to be a very compassionate man, the kind of officer the force could do with having more of. Unlike Roger Clarke. She and Stefan had forged a good friendship back then, even pairing up as badminton partners until Stefan's career took him further up the ladder.

'I wish there was an easy way to say this, Terri.'

Stefan looked unusually grave, and her heart sank. Clarke *had* complained about her. She should have known it.

'I need to ask you a few questions, the first being why were you trying to access information on Nicholas Wentworth? What is your interest in him?'

This wasn't what she'd been expecting, and the warning bells were ringing. 'I have no interest in him per se, Chief. I was just thinking about Operation Mitre, and his name came into my mind. I wondered if he was still such a high-flying magnate these days, that's all. Simple curiosity. I had a real shock when the access denied warning flagged up.'

'And Operation Mitre? You were thinking about that for what reason?'

She stuck as close to the truth as she dared. 'Probably because of Sam Helsdown, sir. His brother's house was burnt down yesterday, and I've been trying to contact either Mike or Sam and let the poor guy know that while he's having a jolly holiday with his family, his home has been reduced to ashes.' She shrugged and gave him a hint of a smile. 'I kind of associated Sam with trouble, I guess, sir, which Operation Mitre certainly was on every count.'

Stefan regarded her intently, as if trying to make up his mind about something. 'And Julia Berkman, Terri? Were your searches about her just kind of associating too?'

Now she was angry. 'Why exactly is my computer history under the microscope, sir? I've done nothing wrong, and the reason I was checking out Julia is because of Sam, the best DS I've ever had, who she's put through the ringer. I wondered where she was and why, all of a sudden, she's seen fit to let the child she's been keeping from him for two years come to stay.'

'Then if that's the truth, you might not understand what I'm about to say. However,' he looked at her steadily, 'I'm afraid it has to be said.' He sighed. 'Terri, I have two ways of handling this. It's your choice.'

Now she was worried. 'Go ahead, although I'm at a loss as to know what on earth can be so serious about a couple of random searches on an office computer.'

Ignoring her comment, he continued, 'You can either go on leave for a fortnight, with immediate effect, or — and it pains me to have to do it — I will have to ask for your warrant card, and you will go directly home for as long as it takes for me to look into this matter.'

'You're suspending me?' she exclaimed. 'But why? Stefan, you know me, I've never stepped out of line in twenty-seven years of policing!'

'As you know, a suspension dos not necessarily result from any formal misconduct. I promise I will make it a priority to investigate what has occurred.'

He was not liking this, she could tell, but he was also in deadly earnest. 'Investigate what? Nothing *has* occurred!' she croaked. 'This is lunacy!'

He leaned even closer and lowered his voice. 'Take the holiday. And stay away from here and from computers in general. Do no more than watch box sets. I'm asking you to do this for your own sake, Terri. This is no small matter, believe me. You are heading into dangerous waters, my friend. Stop swimming right now.'

'What's going on, Stefan?' she whispered. 'Can't you tell me?'

Stefan's demeanour softened. 'Look, Terri, it's because you're a good and loyal officer that I want you well away from this. There's an ongoing situation that is coming to a climax, and it's toxic, believe me. You've inadvertently walked into a minefield and I'm not prepared to allow a good detective to become a casualty. I can't give you the whole story, but it involves a possibly bent cop — and that's only the tip of the iceberg. The investigation itself, with or without this renegade, is massive, and a good outcome is crucial for us.' He stared straight into her eyes. 'Now, forget what I've just said, all right? But do as I say, and go on leave. Don't make me suspend you. Just give me a plausible reason for an unplanned break, and I'll see it's approved without question. Something like a family crisis would be good.'

Nothing came to her. Family crises are fine if you have a family. All she had was one slightly batty elderly aunt. Well, Auntie would have to do. 'Er, I have to attend to some legal matters for my infirm old aunt. She's the last remaining member of the family and no longer capable, physically or mentally, of dealing with the disposition of her family home and possessions. Her solicitor has requested my presence. Will that do?'

'Fine. So, you'll take my advice?' He looked at her for confirmation.

She found it hard to lie, especially to him, but she said, 'I'll go, Stefan. I'll back right off those issues you mentioned, but only because I couldn't face a suspension. There's not too much else going on in my life other than my career. If I lost that, I'd have nothing.'

'And it would be unjust, I'm fully aware of that. When this is all over and I can debrief you fully, you will understand that there is no alternative. It's imperative that you leave the Helsdown brothers, and anything to do with Operation

Mitre, well alone. Don't even speak to Sam Helsdown, and if he rings you, let me know at once. No one else, understand? It's not negotiable, Terri, it's an order.' He smiled faintly. 'I'm remembering what a bloody clever sportswoman you were, Terri Lander, completely focussed on winning the game. You could feign a shot that would fool your opponent into believing it would land in one corner of the court and then send it in the opposite direction. Whatever you do, don't try that kind of manoeuvre here. Lives are at stake, remember that, and if that's not important enough to you, your career is in the same situation.'

Terri swallowed. She was trapped. 'You paint a very clear picture, sir. Meanwhile, I'll stand by Sam Helsdown to the end. I feel as if I'm going to lose something precious no matter what I do.'

'If you do as I ask, you will lose nothing, I promise.'

She saw a message in those words, but she wasn't sure what it was. Worse than that, she was far from sure if she could comply with what Stefan was asking of her.

* * *

At one point in the night, Sam believed he heard the sound of muffled sobs. He was on his way into Sophie's room when he realised it was Mike who was stifling the tears. In all their years growing up together, he had never heard Mike cry. He realised Mike wouldn't want his brother to know — he would be terribly embarrassed, for a start. His pain was a personal thing, too deep to be soothed by a few well-meant platitudes. Sam pretended to be asleep.

They were all quiet over breakfast, and although Mike endeavoured to make a few jokes for Sophie's sake, Sam understood that the gravity of what had happened to his home had really sunk in. It had to be that, or the complexity of what they were mixed up in was just too much for him to comprehend.

While Sophie got washed and dressed, Mike took him aside. 'Look, I have to go home.' He gave a hollow laugh.

'Figuratively, that is. Forget what I said last night, it was the whisky. How am I going to get anything like retribution from people as ruthless and powerful as whoever is after us? But I still have to sort things out — insurance, my business, and all the legal crap. Hell, bro, I'm floundering. All I can think of is going to the police for help.'

Sam felt a stab of fear. 'No, Mike, don't even think like that. You could still be in terrible danger. You have to keep your head down and stay way off their radar. Hang on here with us, there's safety in numbers. Don't go off alone, it's madness. Look what they've done already, and we have no idea why. You can't risk it, and not only that, we need you.'

'The inactivity will drive me mad. I can't sit here and do jigsaws.'

'Then do what you said last night, get on your laptop. We need your expertise. I know you'll make your searches untraceable, so get your head down and find us some answers, find where Julia is. You've been tracking her for years. Carry on doing it.'

Mike looked unconvinced. 'Just remember, these people will have technicians just as skilled as me, maybe considerably more so. If they are the kind of organisation I now suspect them to be, they will also have access to more technology than even I can imagine. Like I said before, there's a chance I could lead them straight here, which is what I possibly did in the first place. Are you prepared to risk your safe place, and maybe that little girl's safety, just to play Hunt the Julia? Shit, Sam, even you don't know which side she's playing for!'

Sam said nothing. Then he groaned. 'No, I guess not. We're just going to have to find ways of keeping Sophie amused and you sane. I'm going to be fully occupied as bodyguard and security operative. Oh, and regarding Julia, I'm working on the old adage, keep your friends close, and your enemies closer.' He gave his brother a friendly punch. 'Hang in there, Mike. When this is sorted, I'll take more time off and help you with all the stuff regarding the fire; we'll look for a new home for you too. Meanwhile, you're so good with

Sophie, why don't you try to find out a bit about her and her gift with figures? She said something a bit odd the other day, and I never followed it up. She said, "I see numbers." What do you think that means?'

To his relief, Mike looked interested. 'Okay, I'll give it a go. And I'll see what else I can get her to tell me about that strange fostering set-up and the other kids. Softly, softly, of course.'

Sam let out a breath he hadn't realised he had been holding. Mike was staying.

CHAPTER EIGHT

Mike felt as if he was at war with himself. Every emotion that welled up was counteracted by its opposite. He wanted out, to run away from this place, but at the same time he needed to feel safe, to stay where he was. He was eaten up with righteous anger one moment, then almost cowed by fear the next. Never in his life had he felt so adrift. He liked order, and now his whole world — what was left of it — was in chaos.

He looked across to where Sophie was staring sadly at the blank screen of her tablet. She looked as bereft as he felt. 'Still no contact, Soph?'

'No, I think it's broken. I miss my homework.' She spoke as if she had lost a puppy.

'You have to be the first kid in the world to utter those words.' Mike smiled, seeing a way in. 'What's so special about maths, Soph?'

She looked up and her expression changed completely. 'It's the numbers. They're just so beautiful.'

'I've never thought of them quite like that,' said Mike, thinking of his tax returns. 'Can you explain what you mean?'

'You know, Uncle Mike, they're so pretty, like names and the days of the week.' She regarded him like a patient teacher with a slow pupil. 'Like Wednesdays are blue. Daddy is green. Numbers are different colours too.'

Mike understood. She was a synesthete! Liz Court, one of his technicians at MH TEC, was the same. It was a fascinating condition, in which an individual's perception of numbers and letters is associated with colour. Liz had explained it as a kind of synergy of the senses — grapheme–colour synaesthesia, she called it. 'I know what you're talking about, Sophie. I have a friend who's the same, but we don't all have that gift. Like, were your friends in Greece the same as you?'

'Oh no, it was just a Sophie thing, like Florence's thing was learning languages, and Jim could tell what was wrong with animals just by looking at them, and they always let him help them — they never bit him or anything.' For a moment she looked sad when she spoke of her lost friends. 'What are you good at, Uncle Mike?'

'Not much,' he admitted. 'Except technology. Like computers, I'm pretty hot with those.'

She handed him her tablet.

After a few moments he handed it back. 'It's not broken, Sophie, but someone has infected it with what we call a virus. It's basically killed all your programs, software, and files, and crashed your system. You won't get any more maths on this, I'm afraid.'

'Who would do a horrible thing like that?' she demanded.

The fucking devious shits who burn down houses and lie to children about their parentage, he thought angrily. 'Bad people. And unfortunately there's quite a lot of those about.' He grinned at her. 'But if you want number puzzles, or even proper mathematical exercises, I can download some to my laptop and you can do them on that if you like?'

She brightened. 'Can you do that?'

'Sure. What's your favourite kind of maths?'

'Anything. Anything with numbers. I just love to watch them.' Her face took on a dreamy expression. 'I guess my favourite is multiplication, but I don't need exercises for that. It just happens.'

'How does that work? If, for instance, I ask you what the square of fifty-six is, how wo—'

'Three thousand one hundred and thirty-six,' she said at once.

Mike had heard of this kind of thing, and he'd watched *Rain Man* twice, but he'd never met anyone who could do it. 'How on earth . . . ?'

Sophie shrugged. 'I just see the first number and its colours, then the second, and they kind of turn into the answer. It's just there, and my tutor said they're never wrong. He checked my solutions over and over, even doing cubing, or raising numbers to maybe the fifth power. They were always right.'

'You can calculate that kind of thing in your head?' Mike was dumbfounded. Raising a number to the fifth power meant taking that number and multiplying it five times over. It was called power multiplication, and again, he'd never heard of anyone capable of doing it.

'I'm not clever, Uncle Mike, because it happens without me doing anything. My tutor said it's spon . . . spont . . . ?'

'Spontaneous?'

She nodded. 'That's it. So, I do all the other maths to learn how to be really clever, and use what I see with my coloured numbers to get the answers.' She smiled a little shyly. 'Most are really easy, that's why I like to do more and more. I want to work with numbers when I grow up, Uncle Mike. They're like my friends, I'm happy with them around me.'

'I think you'll be brilliant,' he said truthfully. *So long as you're allowed to live that long.*

He retrieved his laptop from the bedroom and found a site where Sophie could choose her own exercises. When she was happily working away, he went to look for Sam.

He eventually found his brother in the small patio area at the back of the chalet. Mike stood and watched for a while, trying to work out what he was doing. He seemed to be unwinding a long reel of string.

'Trip wire.' Sam dropped the strong twine almost to ground level and tied it to a fence post. 'Low enough not to be seen and taut enough for a boot to catch it, and,' he pointed to a cluster of precariously balanced flowerpots, 'they should make enough noise to have me up and outside in seconds.' He exhaled. 'Not much, not nearly enough, but this roll of string is all I have to play with, so it's better than nothing, I guess. I've set up three of these, so watch your step, okay?'

'Frightens us half to death and we rush out to meet a badger. Still, it's better than a poke in the eye with a sharp stick. Good for you, bro. Now, listen to this, I've been talking to our Sophie.'

Mike told him what he had learned. Sam had never come across synaesthesia before.

'Neither would I if it hadn't been for my colleague, Liz. She and her sister both have it. Basically it's increased communication between different sensory regions of the brain; it's automatic and quite involuntary. It manifests itself in a number of ways because it's a mix of senses — some people see letters, numbers, and sounds as colours, that's the most common. Others hear sounds when they taste food, or touch an object. There are a whole lot of variables, some very rare.'

'So, Sophie sees numbers in colour, and can manipulate them to provide correct answers to mathematical problems?' Sam shook his head. 'That's bizarre.'

Mike looked at his brother thoughtfully. 'Apart from her ability to calculate, I think she's just wired up very differently. She absorbs mathematical problems like a sponge. I've been watching her, and it's astonishing. She shows no sign of being autistic, but we know so little about her that I'm forced to wonder if she's a savant.'

Sam whistled softly. 'I was told she was priceless.'

'That could well be the case,' Mike said. 'I'm going back inside to see what other little gems I can uncover.'

'Go for it! And put the kettle on, it's brass monkeys out here. I'll be in shortly.'

Mike hurried back into the chalet, feeling a lot less hopeless than he had at breakfast. With each new revelation, little Sophie Whoever-she-was became more of an enigma, and it became all the more important to keep her safe.

* * *

Stefan Ellwood knew who the caller would be before he answered the phone.

The speaker's tone was clipped, officious. 'Has the matter been dealt with, Detective Chief Superintendent?'

Stefan was similarly business-like. 'It is, sir. My officer is no longer operational.'

'Good. Please make quite sure that there is no more interference. It will not be tolerated. No one — and I repeat, no one — will escape the axe if this project should fail. Do I make myself clear?'

'Perfectly, sir.'

'Then carry on.' The phone hummed as the caller disconnected.

Stefan swore and put the phone down. He and two other contacts had spent two years working as a tight-knit team, striving to clear up the wreckage left by Operation Mitre. Now this man had taken over, just as they were near to closing down an undercover operation that had been running for over a decade. In Stefan's eyes, this high-ranking officer was a heartless, soulless machine, a man to be avoided whenever possible.

He had several other important calls to make, and a couple of visits to certain key people, but before he did anything, he closed his eyes for a moment, silently willing Terri to do as he'd asked. If she didn't, there was a good chance that they'd both be queuing at the Job Centre by this time next week.

* * *

Before Sam could get back indoors, his phone rang. It was Terri Lander, on her covert PAYG phone. She sounded unusually tense.

'Sam, listen, I've been removed from the station. Not suspended, but I was *that* close. If it had been anyone other than DCI Ellwood, my warrant card would be locked in a desk drawer in HQ by now.'

'Jesus, Terri! Are you okay?'

'Shell-shocked and pretty pissed off, but yeah, okay for now. But listen, you have to do something, and fast. It could even be too late, but you've missed something bloody important, Detective.'

Sam stiffened. 'Like what?'

'I have no idea if I'm correct here but take precautions anyway. Our own people are mixed up in this mess. They have to be, or they would never have hit me this hard. Sam, it's your mobile phone. They can track you! You keep it switched on in case you need to be contacted again, don't you? But think about it. We can easily find where a phone is located from the signal. We do it all the time.'

His heart sank. 'Oh my God! I was so anxious to watch for warning calls, I didn't even think! Shit, Terri! Anyone can track a cell phone, not just the police. Hackers do it all the time, and you can even get free mobile tracking apps these days. Where was my head?'

'Overload, my friend. Even top cops can't think of everything when they're under the kind of pressure you are. But rather than debate this, the moment I hang up, switch off, take the batteries out of your phone, then drive to the nearest supermarket and grab a burner phone. Put the numbers you will need in the contacts, then I suggest you pack your own phone into a padded envelope — you can get one in the store — and post it to me for safekeeping. You know my address.'

For a moment he thought he would panic. The full extent of the emotional stress he was under hit him like a train. Fear for his daughter's safety, and the onus on him to protect another precious child, while watching his beloved brother's life get decimated, had clouded his thinking. Just the night before, they had been talking about the Wi-Fi in the cabin being safe to use as it was in Ryan's name. Even then, he hadn't twigged. 'If my stupid rookie mistake costs that child her safety, I'll never forgive myself. All I can say is thank you, Terri, I can't tell you how much I appreciate it, but now, please, please, pull out of this mess. I don't want to have to start worrying about you too. I'm asking you not to contact me, unless it's life or death for,' he nearly said Sophie, 'my daughter.'

He couldn't help smiling at Terri's final comment: 'Bollocks!'

Back inside the cabin, he found a delighted Sophie working her way through reams of figures on Mike's laptop. Lost in her own world, she didn't even see him come in. He beckoned to his brother and they went into the kitchen area, out of her hearing. There, he told Mike what Terri had said.

'I don't believe it!' Mike closed his eyes then groaned softly. 'Even I should have worked that out. I trace phones all the time for some of our clients — official bodies, like you guys. Fuck. Does this mean we up sticks and move on? Or what?'

'I really don't know, Mike. I'll do what Terri suggested and get a burner phone as soon as possible. I'm just not sure how.' He felt torn. 'I daren't leave you two, and I really don't want to risk leaving this place unattended.'

'How far away is the nearest supermarket?' asked Mike.

'Fifteen, maybe twenty minutes.'

'Give me directions and the address to post your phone to. I'll go, so long as you don't mind me driving your car. You stay with Sophie. I can be back in an hour.'

Again, Sam was uncertain. 'I don't want you out there alone either, Mike.'

'Come on! Even I don't know where I am! How do you expect someone else to find me? One hour, that's all. I won't start browsing the shelves for a tasty beef Wellington or a bottle of ten-year-old malt, I promise. I'll by a cheap phone, a packet of Jiffy bags and a book of stamps. Then I'll shove it in the nearest postbox, end of story.' Mike stood up. 'I'll finish my tea and go. No arguments.'

'Listen, Mike, and don't take offence, but you have no idea how to shake off a tail. Suppose you're spotted, you could bring someone right back here.' After his earlier oversight, Sam didn't want to miss a thing. 'The problem is, I don't have a better idea. I could disable my phone and not bother with a burner, but that leaves us too vulnerable. With no phone at all, we'd be scuppered if anything serious happened. Sure, we could send an email to Terri from your laptop, but only if we have plenty of time. In an emergency we'd be stuffed!' He frowned at Mike. 'I'm sorry to say this, but I think we have to move on, though I have no idea where. I mean, someone could be heading our way right now.' As he spoke, Sam began to sense impending danger. 'We're not safe here, Mike. Get your things together, including that laptop. I'll get Sophie's clothes and my few bits. Load the car. Forget the food and everything else. Essentials only, and hurry.'

Mike drained his mug and went immediately to their room. Through the open door, Sam caught sight of him stuffing his lucky Smurf into his bag. Sam hoped it would work its magic, this time for all of them.

* * *

Terri Lander was taking stock of her life. It didn't take long. By now there was little left to reckon with.

She began by listing the failures. As a daughter. Failure as a wife, a mother. Excelled as a police officer, with her commendation to prove it, but at what cost? Her career had been a success, and probably still would be if Roger Clarke hadn't turned up, along with a new breed of officers that were filtering insidiously into CID. Stefan Ellwood was the only man of rank she actually still respected. Now even more so.

She raised her arms above her head, stretched and let out a sigh. But he was also another problem. What should she do about Stefan? She was no fool, and she knew he had risked a lot to warn her the way he had. He might even have compromised himself by allowing her to keep her warrant card. The last thing she wanted was to dump him in the slurry, and if there was any other way, she'd take it, but . . .

Terri stared at the map on her computer screen. Saltire Lakes. Of course.

She smiled a little sadly. Thinking about it in retrospect, she hadn't really needed that GPS tracker to find out where Sam was hiding. He'd probably forgotten that it was she who'd suggested the cabins by the lakes in the first place. He had thanked her for the recommendation at the time, but since he'd never mentioned them again, she had assumed he wasn't interested. She knew he had somewhere he went to when he needed a break, but hadn't realised where it was until this moment.

So, she knew where he was, but what should she do next? As far as she could see, people would get hurt no matter what she chose to do. She supposed it was inevitable if you got involved in something as big and corrupt as what was going on right now — and had been for a good long while, it seemed.

For Terri had begun to get an idea of the bigger picture, and she didn't like what she was seeing. But she was aware that a little knowledge is a dangerous thing. She closed her eyes and took a deep breath. She was about to make a crucial decision.

She stood up and began to pace. She'd always done her best for Queen and country. She had never broken the oath she'd made to protect life and property. She had always endeavoured to serve her community well. She had an impressive arrest rate, and still did, including the recent raid, in which they had netted more drugs than they could ever have expected, and had seen two serious players escorted to the custody suite.

So, if this was where it all ended, so be it. Right now, she was going to help a friend in need, and sod the rest.

CHAPTER NINE

While Mike threw everything they needed into the car, Sam put the batteries back into his phone and checked the messages one last time. After all, if they were already onto his hiding place, activating the phone for a minute or two couldn't make things any worse. He waited impatiently for it to connect. Then he stared at it. He had three messages, all from an unrecognised number, and all said the same: *Stay where you are!*

Sam let out a noisy breath and stared at his phone. Was this a genuine warning? Or a trap?

'Daddy, what's wrong?' Sophie was tugging at his sleeve.

'I wish I knew, sweetheart,' he murmured.

Mike appeared in the doorway. 'Everything's in, so come on!'

Sam held out the phone to Mike. 'Any ideas? Because I don't.'

Mike read the messages and puffed out his cheeks. 'Fu—' He stopped himself, remembering Sophie. 'Er, a rock and a hard place springs to mind. What does your gut tell you?'

Sam suddenly understood something, although he couldn't have put it into words. 'We get out! Now!' He turned to Sophie. 'Come on, angel. I'm going to show you a few pointers from my police pursuit driving course.'

As Mike bundled Sophie into the waiting car, Sam decommissioned his phone, then hurried after them, locking the door. He didn't know why, but he was certain those messages were not from Julia, and if they were, then she truly was not the person he had believed her to be.

The moment Mike had asked the question, he knew they were under threat. Any second, the peace of this lakeside setting could be shattered, possibly with terrible consequences for one, if not all of them.

Sam didn't tear off at breakneck speed. He inched carefully forward, watching for any sign of unwanted company. He had a choice of two ways out — a direct one, the track that led to the lane in, or a loop that circled the lake and met the junction at the entrance. He chose the circular route. He had seen no movement at either of the other cabins, and had watched them ever since becoming aware of his mistake in leaving his phone switched on. Anyone panicking would make a mad dash for the exit, which would therefore be where their attackers would wait for them.

He could hear Mike breathing in the back seat. He too would be on the lookout for the slightest sign of danger.

'It's very quiet,' Mike murmured.

'Let's hope it stays that way.'

He chose one of the other cabins, which was rarely used. He pulled up under a car port that also served as a home for the dustbins and a small stack of logs. From there he could see along to the next cabin, while being hidden from the lake and the track in.

'I don't think there is anyone on this side of the lake,' he whispered almost to himself, omitting the word 'yet'. Even so, a sense of something untoward still permeated the place. What he really wanted to do was go ahead on foot and scout out the area by the entrance. One glance at the pale face at his side told him that was not going to happen. Sam Helsdown was going nowhere if it meant leaving this child.

He took a small pair of binoculars from the tray between the front seats, noiselessly opened the car door and stood beside it. All he could hear was the sound of blackbirds squabbling somewhere close by.

Leaving the door open, he moved over to the corner of the car port and staying well back, trained the binoculars on the far side of the lake and in the direction of the entrance.

Just as he was about to give up and return to the car, Sam tensed up. Had something stirred there, between the trees? He moved the glasses very slowly backwards and forwards. There was another slight disturbance a little further away. And another. A touch of colour that didn't belong in nature, a kind of metallic grey, as in vehicle paint.

He felt a shiver zip between his shoulder blades. It could be nothing suspicious, possibly the manager of the site who called in every week. Or it could be something far more sinister. Given the circumstances, Sam knew which of those two options his money was on.

He thought quickly. If there was more than one vehicle up by the entrance, he would be driving straight into their hands, and there was no other way out of the site. Well, not by car, but he knew something probably no one else did.

Ducking back into the car, he whispered urgently, 'Get out, you two. And do it silently. No slamming the doors — push them to, but no noise, understand?'

Looking terrified, Sophie did as she was told. The moment she was out, Sam put an arm firmly around her shoulder. 'We're going somewhere on foot, kiddo, and I want you to tread as lightly as a fairy. Watch out for dry branches, they crack quite loudly. Can you do that?'

She nodded and swallowed.

Mike rolled his eyes. The thought of treading like a fairy when you are built like a scrum half obviously didn't hold much water.

'Come on then, follow me. I'll lead, Sophie next, and, Mike, you keep your eyes and ears peeled from the rear.'

Sam knew exactly where he was going. He just hoped his abandoned car didn't attract attention too soon. He didn't want anyone tracking their footsteps, not that he thought they would, as there was no apparent way out of the site without taking to the fields, where they would be spotted immediately.

As they forged forward through the scrubby wood that surrounded the cabins, he gave thanks for the incident of the lost dog. Without this small drama which had unfolded on his last trip here, he would have had no idea of where to go to hide Sophie from whoever was after her.

A couple named James and Anita, who rented the cabin where he had left his car, had been there at the same time as him. They had brought with them a young rescue dog, a skinny version of a springer spaniel that they told him was a Spanish Breton. It was a skittish little dog, very friendly, and although generally very good on the lead, if let off, its recall clearly needed more work. On this occasion, it had bolted from the cabin through a slightly open door. Sam had heard them calling for it and had gone to help. Seeing a flash of white and tan flying through the wood, he had given chase, and seen the dog's furiously wagging tail disappear through a gap in the high ivy-covered wall of the perimeter boundary. He had squeezed through after it and found himself in the grounds of the old abbey.

So, thanks to a naughty dog named Diego, he knew exactly where to take his precious ward and hide her.

As they hurried towards his secret entrance to the deserted old building, he cursed the fact that he had bought Sophie a pink coat. Right now, a nice dreary camouflage colour would have been preferable — she stood out like a beacon against the dark green foliage and brown bracken. In a whisper he told her to stop. 'Take off your coat, honey, and put it on inside out. If it gets messed up, I'll buy you another one, but pink is not a great colour for keeping a low profile.'

They pressed on, keeping as quiet as they could. Sam didn't think the others had heard the soft growl of an engine, maybe more than one. He speeded up just a little, now fully convinced that whoever he had been asked to protect Sophie from was somewhere along the track to the cabins.

Once they were through and into the parkland beyond the lakes, Sam felt a little easier. From the road, and from the fields that surrounded the old abbey estate, it looked impenetrable. A stone wall circumnavigated the whole area, and the front gates, great rusting iron things, were locked and secured with a chain and a padlock. The manager of the lakes site had told him there had been grand plans for the place, but the finding of some old archives dating from the fifteen hundreds had thrown a spanner in the works, and all the proposed renovations had been halted. A useless piece of trivia floated into Sam's head about some abbot being reprimanded for owning 'villages, churches and serfs', following which stringent measures had been put in place to prevent the accruing of profits for monetary gain other than what was due to the church.

Now the place was a mass of crumbling stonework, the remains of the abbey's church, cloister and dormitories still giving some indication of their layout and structure. There were other buildings, still more or less as they were, stables, barns and service buildings, along with a recognisable gatehouse. The Abbey House itself had been rebuilt several times through the ages and now stood, neglected but proud, shut up tightly against resourceful squatters, vandals and urban explorers. Not that it kept these last out, Sam guessed, but they did no damage, merely taking photographs and recording what they found. They came and went, leaving no trace of their presence.

However, it was not the main house that interested Sam. He had found the runaway spaniel inside a small stone building that was comparatively well preserved, with the remains of some small arched windows that gave a good view of the gatehouse. It would provide cover and protection while allowing him to watch for unwanted visitors.

Inside, he felt able to relax slightly.

'What is this place?' whispered Mike, staring out of one of the windows.

'An old Cistercian abbey. I'm relying on the fact that whoever is looking for us will assume we are either hiding in one of the other cabins, or trying to make our way out by road. Hopefully, they won't think to look for us here. I've checked before, out of curiosity, and there's no easy access at all.'

Mike made no comment, probably for the sake of Sophie, although he didn't seem convinced. Sam looked at the little girl who had sat herself on a stone bench at the back of the storeroom. She had hugged herself tightly and was rocking slightly.

'Don't be frightened, Sophie,' he said in his softest voice. He went and sat next to her. For once she looked even younger than her ten years.

'But I am frightened.' She looked at him, her expression confused and anxious. 'I don't understand what's going on.'

You and me both, he thought darkly. 'I'm sorry this is all so scary for you, but we have to try to be brave until someone comes to help us.'

'Julia?'

'Maybe, or other people who want to keep you safe.' He gazed down at her, trying to look reassuring. 'We will get some answers soon, and then we'll both understand why we're in this mess.'

The look Mike flashed him said, '*There's a pig flying over!*'

He returned his attention to Sophie. 'Okay, so what do you usually do to make yourself feel better if you get a bit stressed out?'

'I count.'

'That's good. So why not close your eyes and visualise your coloured numbers? Let Uncle Mike and me do the worrying for a bit.'

Although the rocking didn't stop, she closed her eyes. Soon she was reciting numbers under her breath.

While he and Mike watched, Sophie seemed to relax and the rocking became gentle and rhythmic. She was speaking the names of numbers as others would the words of a beautiful poem, and he could almost see the colours as each one rolled off her tongue.

'What's she doing?' he whispered.

'Reciting pi,' Mike said. 'She's memorised all the different values of pi.'

'Ten-year-olds do that?'

'Oh yes, they even have competitions. Don't you ever watch YouTube?'

Sam shook his head, 'Not for things like that. Sorry, you know me and figures. I never liked maths, I didn't understand it.'

Mike kept his eyes on Sophie. 'Pi is the mathematical constant that represents the ratio of a circle's circumference to its diameter . . . oh, never mind, the important thing is that she's calm.'

She was, and Sam felt free to try and work out their next move. 'Try' being the operative word. He had managed to get them away from immediate danger to a place of comparative safety, but what next? It was afternoon, and soon it would be getting dark. This could be a help; it could also be hazardous in the extreme. One thing was for sure, this little girl couldn't spend the whole night here in the cold and the dark. Whatever he chose to do needed to be done well before then.

Automatically, he patted his coat pocket for reassurance. He was wearing a lined parka with several deep pockets, and in the most accessible was the Glock pistol. He hoped he'd never have to use it, but for the sake of that child, he knew he would if he had to.

* * *

Terri Lander was slowing down at the approach to Saltire Lakes when she saw another vehicle driving in ahead. Her hackles rose. Her years on the force had taught her to almost instinctively recognise both official vehicles and those used by villains. The dark 4x4 that had driven into that lane looked like a cross between the two. Special ops? Heavyweight criminals? Could be either, but it certainly wasn't Fred and Mabel with a picnic lunch!

Terri continued past the turning, pulled into a lay-by on the other side of the road and pretended to be using her mobile phone. A few moments later a second equally business-like vehicle drove in after the first. So she was not the first to arrive at the party.

Terri swore under her breath. What the hell was Sam up against in there? More to the point, *who* was he up against? Not that it mattered right now. It was time she waded in and lent a hand, because as far as she could gauge, there was only one set of good guys in this weird scenario — Sam and Mike.

She quickly made a mental check of everything she might need, thankful that she was warmly dressed in thick cargo pants, a Barbour and hiking boots. Having no idea of what might be asked of her there was little she could prepare for, but she had two ace cards. The first she played before she left her car. She pulled out her phone and rang a number that she hadn't used in years.

He answered immediately and let her speak without interrupting.

She spoke fast. 'You know far more about this than I do but what I do know is that we have a serving officer and two members of the public, one a ten-year-old girl, in grave danger. I'll give you the location, but use only the best, and make quite sure you have an armed unit with you. Silent approach, one hit on the blues and twos and you could start a war that could kill a little kid. I'm going to observe and report back. Keep your line free for me.'

He accepted what she said without question, not that she'd expected anything else, but he insisted she wait for them before going in. She should remember everything he'd told her because it involved matters she wasn't aware of. One wrong move on her part could prove catastrophic for everyone involved.

She said she was fully aware that she was being kept in the dark — not unusual where the higher echelons were involved — but he would have to trust her to do whatever she saw fit should a life be in danger. She then gave him the exact location and ended the call. He would know she'd disobey his instruction to wait. She couldn't, not when a fellow officer needed assistance.

She locked her car, and making sure no further vehicles were arriving to join the two she'd seen, ran across the road, but away from the sign that pointed to Saltire Lakes, towards the wall that circumnavigated the old abbey next door. She had one small job to do before she could enter the woodland area that led to the cabins.

It didn't take long, and then she was back close to the entrance, making sure that her way was free of men in expensive cars.

Modern phones that could be tracked using GPS were so accurate she even knew which cabin was Sam's, so she turned quickly into the lane leading to the lakes, then left it as soon as possible and made her way there through the woods.

This was her other ace card. She knew this place like the back of her hand. She had played here as a child, long before the cabins were put up by her brother when their father died and left him the land. The reason she had suggested the log cabin to Sam was because not only did she know it would be exactly the right place for a bolthole, but also that her brother would charge him a fair rent. Win-win, Sam!

She moved silently through the woods, praying with every step that Sam had his policeman's head on and been aware that something bad was afoot. His emotions and the intense stress he was under had already allowed him to commit one serious and uncharacteristic error. Now she hoped he was back in the zone, and had decamped already.

Five minutes later she found his empty cabin. Trying to follow his thought processes, she soon found his unlocked car in his neighbour's car port. She nodded thoughtfully. He hadn't locked it, so he must have wanted to avoid the beep of the locking system, plus its flashing light. That told her that he was aware of the danger they were in. *Good boy, Sam, you're on your toes and away from here, but where?* As far as she knew, he had two options. One was to hide until he saw that whoever was after them had noticed the abandoned car, then, when they had gone, return to it and drive like the wind to the exit in the hope that they hadn't blocked it. It would be far too risky to chance that with a child in the car. That left option two, the one she favoured. It all depended on whether Sam had bothered to explore the place during his previous visits, and whether he was curious about ruined buildings.

Terri smiled to herself. She knew Sam pretty well. He would definitely have worked out that option two was the safest for his daughter. She'd put good money on the fact that he had found a way in.

That settled, all she had to do was find him.

CHAPTER TEN

Sam's head was a shed, which was the term his father used when he felt totally confused or overwhelmed by unwanted thoughts. *Yeah, a head full of crap*, he thought, *and not one sensible idea among them.* Every course of action he came up with had a downside. His latest idea had been to activate his phone and ring Terri, or even the station, for help. The downside was not knowing what or who was on the other side of that wall. He could be asking his friend, or his comrades, to walk into a bloodbath. Over everything hung the fact that someone considered Sophie to be a priceless child, which meant they'd use desperate measures to get hold of her. His phone remained out of service.

They had been there for almost half an hour, hearing no sounds or other indications of being followed into the abbey grounds. Sophie was now perfectly calm, although she was still wandering in a world made up of numbers and colours. Sam would have liked to have joined her — the real world wasn't looking too good right now.

'How long before they decide that we must have made it to the road and hitched a lift out of here?' asked Mike edgily. 'Or will they? If it was me hunting runaways, I'd check out the neighbouring property, which means right here.'

'Normally I'd agree, but even you would find it nigh on impossible to get over that wall, Mike, so a little kid would never be able to. And there's no other way in than through those gates, and it would take a tank to bulldoze those down. We are as safe as we can be, all things considered. As to time, well, who knows? I'd like to make a move pretty soon, but they might keep watching my car until nightfall. They could think we'll sneak back to the car under cover of darkness and try to drive out.' The look he gave his brother was full of anguish. 'All I want to do is keep Sophie safe, and I have no idea how.'

Before he could say anything else, he noticed that Mike's expression had changed. His brother was staring through one of the windows in the direction of the gatehouse.

Mike didn't move. 'I think something's going on at the gates, Sam, but it's too far away to see properly. Have you got your binoculars?'

Sam pulled them out of his pocket and trained them on the gates. Nothing was clear, twilight had come early and shadows obscured his view, but Mike was right. Something was happening. He saw vague figures moving about and the outline of at least one car. Sam gritted his teeth. He needed to know what was going on down there. Only then could he make the decision he'd been struggling with.

'Stay here with Sophie, Mike, keep her close to you. I'm going to scout out what's occurring down there. I'll be back in minutes, that's all. I'll skirt along the back of the ruins until I'm close enough to get a better view.'

Without waiting for an answer, he slipped out of the old store and melted into the shadows of the ruined abbey.

In no time he was close enough for his binoculars to give him a proper look, and what he saw was not good. A dark-coloured Jeep Grand Cherokee with smoky glass windows was blocking the entrance. He watched a man take some serious bolt cutters from the back and hand them to a second man. He ascertained that there were at least four people, and their attention was focussed on the thick chain that secured the iron gates.

It was time to get Sophie out of here!

As he slipped soundlessly from the shelter of one ruined wall to another, he sensed movement close to him. Sam pulled the gun from his pocket and dropped to one knee.

'Relax, Helsdown, you plank!' the familiar voice hissed. 'And don't point a gun at a senior officer, it's not good form.'

He heaved a sigh of relief. 'Terri! But how . . . ?'

'Shut up, talk later, we need to act. Now let's get your daughter out of this mausoleum.' She hurried off ahead of him.

Oh God, he had so much to explain to her!

Terri's presence galvanised Sam. He shoved all peripheral thoughts to the back of his mind, focussed on the job at hand and caught her up. Sticking close to the ruins, they made their way back to the stone storeroom where his brother and Sophie were waiting anxiously.

He noticed Terri give Sophie a strange look, but now was not the time for questions and they both knew it.

'You came in by the breach in the old wall?' Terri asked him urgently.

He wondered how the hell she knew about it, but pushed the question to the back of his mind. 'Yes, it's the only way in from the lakes.'

'No, it isn't, so you need to follow me, the faster the better.' Terri looked from one to the other of them. 'And keep noise to the minimum. They are closer than I hoped they'd be.' She peered out cautiously, then beckoned to them. 'This way. Stay close. We're making for the Abbey House.'

It was still not quite dark, but the magic hour so beloved of photographers was well over and dusk had made everything look blurred and shadowy. The place now seemed far more menacing than it had.

It was a relatively short distance, but it seemed to take an eon. The site had fallen into ruin over the years and it was strewn with debris, natural and manmade, making it difficult to negotiate.

Finally, close to the house itself, Terri held up a hand. They gathered round her to listen.

'At the side of the old Abbey House there is a covered way,' she whispered. 'It leads from the kitchen to an old wooden door in the wall — tradesmen used it for deliveries. That's where we're heading.'

'I never saw that,' muttered Sam.

'You wouldn't. It's covered in ivy and invisible from the lane. Now, come on.'

They were off again, moving along a mossy path between overgrown shrubs, small trees and straggling plants that grew in a tangle at the back of the old house.

As they edged around the corner to the side of the property, they saw the structure Terri had mentioned. It ran for about fifty feet from house to boundary wall, rather like a long stretch of pergola with strong wooden posts supporting cross rafters covered by a thick thatch of wisteria and ivy.

'I freed the gate earlier,' Terri said softly, 'and I left it slightly ajar for a swift exit.'

This next part was the most risky, Sam realised. Although the covered way was shadowy, it did have open sides and they would be visible, and hence vulnerable, for a short time.

Terri was speaking again. 'It comes out onto the farm lane that meets the main road just a few yards further down. My car is in a lay-by on the other side of the road. I suggest we get out of here and you guys hide in the bushes close to the wall, then I'll get the car and pick you up. We could have company when we get outside, Sam, a team and an armed unit could already be in place. I rang this in, but I have no clue about timing.'

'The cavalry? Oh God, I hope so.' Sam was tired of being Sophie's lone protector.

'Okay, let's go. Remember, we use stealth not speed.'

After one of the most daunting few hundred metres he had ever travelled, at last they reached the ancient wooden gate. Terri opened it, lifted the curtain of ivy that had hidden it so well, and they emerged through the bushes onto a wide grass verge.

He was just about to heave an enormous sigh of relief when he took an involuntary step back, holding Sophie tight. All four of them froze.

Bright lights coming from the side of the path blinded him momentarily. Three figures emerged, barring any attempt at escape.

Shock and, although he hated to admit it, fear immobilised him for a few seconds. Then the adrenalin kicked in, and he felt nothing but anger and a fierce determination to protect the girl at all costs.

'Give us the child,' one of them called out.

He stared in horror at the central figure. It was a woman. Julia.

He blinked, and a glint of light on metal told him she held a pistol. It was trained on him.

'Sorry to disappoint you, Sam.'

Her voice was cold as ice, sending shivers down his spine. Then anger turned to hate.

'I said, give us the child. Now.'

'Go fuck yourself, bitch!' He pushed Sophie around behind him. His rage threatened to boil over, destroying all the memories, all the belief in her he had been holding onto for so many years. The tie was broken.

'Cut the histrionics. You have a simple choice. Hand her over and live. Play the hero, and as all three of you are expendable . . .' She gave a chilly laugh. 'You choose.'

'Actually, I'll choose, if you don't mind.'

Before he could stop her, Terri was between him and Sophie and their three adversaries.

What happened next unfolded in a series of still pictures. One of the men flanking Julia raised his arm. There was a loud report, followed by a grunt, Terri jolted back a fraction with the impact, then pitched forward onto the ground.

Sam opened his mouth to shout out in horror, but what happened next took the breath from him.

Two more shots rang out almost simultaneously, one from further away, but the other had come from Julia's pistol.

The two men on either side of her fell to the ground and lay still. Julia remained standing.

Sam watched, dumbfounded, as she put her head back, closed her eyes for a second or two, then exhaled loudly. 'Not quite textbook, but close enough.' A weary smile appeared on her face. 'You can get up now, DI Lander. Bruised ribs, probably, but you'll be able to post a five-star review on Trustpilot for that bulletproof vest.'

Sam was dimly aware of Terri dragging herself to her feet, swearing copiously, clutching at her chest and groaning. 'Hell, but that hurts!'

Around him he vaguely noticed cars, blue lights, uniformed men and women moving forward out of the darkness and into the glare of the headlights. Men, probably from the vehicles used to transport Julia and the two others, were handcuffed, and led to the waiting police vans.

While it all unfolded around him, he stood, clutching the little girl tightly to him. Barely aware that Mike too had his hand resting on Sophie's shoulder, he fervently hoped she'd seen little of what had just happened.

'You were in on this?' he croaked to Terri.

'Not sodding likely,' she growled. 'No more than you were. I think we might be owed a fucking big explanation, Sam Helsdown, don't you? I get the feeling we've been right royally shafted.'

'You'll be debriefed, don't worry about that.' Julia was standing next to them. 'But right now, our main priority is this beautiful child.' She stooped and gently turned Sophie's face to hers. 'Hello, Sophie.'

'Julia! I knew you'd come.' Her face flooded with joy at the sight of her friend, and she pulled away from Sam's grasp and hugged her tightly. After a few moments, she turned back to Sam. 'Daddy, isn't this wonderful?'

'Yes, sweetheart,' he murmured, 'just wonderful.' His emotions were threatening to erupt with a violence that would put Vesuvius to shame, but he shook his head and said nothing.

'We will talk, Sam, but right now, Sophie has to come with me. There are some very important people waiting to hear that she is safe. Then she needs to be cared for by specialist professionals, as we have a lot to tell her.'

'Can Daddy come? Please?' Sophie asked.

'You'll see Sam later, darling, I promise.' She smiled reassuringly. 'Don't worry, you'll be safe with me.'

She will, thought Sam. *Julia's as cool as a cucumber despite having just shot a man dead.* An insane laugh threatened to escape from his throat but he managed to swallow it. If he were to laugh now, he might never stop.

Julia, with Sophie clutching her hand tightly, turned to walk away, then she looked back. 'Thank you, Sam. You really were the only person I could trust. And I meant what I said about talking. We will, and soon.'

'Fine,' he said flatly. 'But just answer me one question. What about Zoe?'

'Safe. Always was, always will be.'

By now the police vehicles had driven away and the drama came to a close. Mike sank down onto the grass. 'Jesus! All I want to do is go home, but I don't fucking have one.'

'You can have Sophie's room,' said Sam glumly. 'I reckon our little guest has gone for good.'

'Very kind of you, brother, but I think I'll check into the nearest luxury hotel, and there I'll stay until I get this godawful mess sorted out.'

'And I need painkillers,' groaned Terri. 'I think I've got a bust rib,' she winced, 'or two, or three.'

Sam stared at her. 'You were wearing a bulletproof vest?'

She lifted up her jacket and showed him.

'Where the hell did you get that from? That's not a standard stabby.'

'Dead right it's not, or I'd be sodding history!' She sighed. 'Remember the drugs haul you missed out on? I heard there could be some pretty heavy protection in place and it could get nasty. A name was mentioned, someone I know carries more than a knife in his pocket. Since I thought you and I would be leading the raid from the front, I invested in two ballistic level 111A vests — one each.' She gave him a weak grin. 'I only put it on because I had no idea what you'd got yourself muddled up in, but I can highly recommend their efficacy.'

He was about to comment when he saw three officers walking towards them. Two he didn't recognise, the other was Chief Superintendent Ellwood. 'Are we finally going to get some answers?' he said softly to Terri.

'I very much doubt it. It's not their way,' muttered Terri. 'I suspect it'll be a grilling and a bollocking, which would be far more par for the course.'

Stefan Ellwood ran his gaze over the motley gathering. 'There is a car waiting to take you to the station. If you would all come with me, please?'

Like we have a choice, thought Sam. He suddenly felt very, very tired.

* * *

It was after midnight when Sam and Mike were handed the new key for his damaged front door and were driven back to his flat. It felt odd being without Sophie. In their brief time together, they seemed to have made such an epic journey. Sam realised that he missed her.

Mike had agreed to stay that night before seeking out a hotel suite and a quality chef, and Sam was grateful. He didn't relish the thought of being alone.

So they sat, as so often before, two glasses and a bottle of malt on the table between them. As neither had a car — Mike's being a burnt-out skeleton in the police pound and Sam's still sitting in a car port at Saltire Lakes — their glasses were considerably fuller than on those previous occasions.

Mike took a long, slow swallow, closed his eyes and exhaled. 'They told me that — and I quote — "my present problems and inconveniences would be taken care of expediently and in their entirety."' He raised his eyebrows. 'So long as I signed a document stating that my lips would remain sealed forever.' He looked at Sam. 'Is this how the police work these days? Is this what you do? Cover up and shut up?'

'Those weren't the police, Mike. They were special operatives — spooks to you. Defence of the realm and all that.' He had known this the moment he saw the two men with the chief, and the way Julia and the child were driven from the area escorted by what he knew to be armoured cars — one in front and one behind.

'Will we ever know what really happened, Sam? I keep wondering about that incredible little girl.'

'No, not officially. When you signed that paper, you effectively blotted out three days of your life and everyone concerned with them. It never happened.' He raised his glass and gave his brother a mischievous smile. 'But I'll be told — unofficially.'

'Julia?' Mike said doubtfully.

'She will tell me the truth this time, I know it.' He smiled affectionately at his brother. 'And you, more than anyone, have earned the right to hear what she says. But it must remain between the two of us.'

'Don't worry about that. This is one part of my life that I will be happy to consign to the past, as quickly as possible. I want to make a new start, but before I set off, I'd really like to know the fate of that child. I'm also intrigued to hear more about that odd set-up in Greece, with those foster carers. Hell, they still have two children in that compound, or whatever it is. What will their fate be?' He took a gulp of his whisky. 'Oh, I was perfectly willing to put my signature to that document. Even my hotel bill will be taken care of, apparently. So tomorrow night it's fillet steak and a nice bottle of something very expensive.'

Sam laughed. 'Go for it. You deserve it.'

'So, what about you, Sam? Where now? Can you and Terri simply walk back into that CID room and take up where you left off, investigating thefts and hunting drug dealers? Writing reports and drinking terrible coffee? After all this?'

'I could, Mike. We've had difficult cases before. We do what we can, then we parcel them off to the CPS, and pray they don't flush all our hard work down the pan. Then we move on to the next case.' He tapped his nail against the crystal glass and listened to it ring. 'The problem is, this one was personal, and it's making me reconsider what I really want out of life. So the answer to your question is that I'll tell you after I've talked to Julia. I'm making no decisions till then. Anyway, I'm on leave at the moment, until I'm fully debriefed and the internal inquiry is closed.' He looked over his glass at his brother. 'I thought you might like a hand with your house-hunting.'

Mike nodded. 'I'd like that, and while we are on the subject, I've been wondering if you'd like to quit this dive and come and share with me? We could get something that would accommodate our two separate lifestyles under one roof. The business is thriving, Sam. It looks like nameless people will be hurrying my insurance claim through, so I can afford the best, and you aren't on your uppers either. Give it a thought?'

'You really are looking for new beginnings, aren't you?' Sam was seeing his brother in a different light since his ordeal. 'Yes, I'll certainly give it some thought. Thanks for the offer, I appreciate it.'

'I was also thinking that you might be getting to see Zoe more often now, so don't you think it would be good to have somewhere a little more, er, salubrious for her to stay in?' He glanced at the shabby décor and the thin carpet. 'No offence, mate, but this place is hardly the Ritz.'

He was right. It was down at heel, and Sam had hardly noticed. It certainly wasn't a proper home, just somewhere to get his head down, eat and generally slob about between shifts. Zoe certainly deserved better. 'You do have a point, Mike. You really do.'

The day grew to a close. They sat on, drinking their whisky, going over everything that had happened, while Sam came to a decision. Whatever he decided to do, Mike should not be the only person looking forward to a new beginning.

* * *

Terri was just considering a long soak in deep, very hot water, when her doorbell rang. She looked at the clock and saw that it was approaching half past twelve. *Oh Lord, what now?* She looked out of the lounge window and saw the familiar tall figure of Stefan Ellwood.

She opened the door and stood back. 'To be honest, I think I might have had enough of you right now, Stefan. But I guess you'd better come in.'

He accepted the drink she offered and they sat in her lounge. He looked around. 'You have a beautiful home, Terri, I've always thought that. You have a great eye for colour and a flair for style.'

'I need a little beauty around me when I get home after a grotty day at the nick. It's my safe place, clean and tidy, unlike some of our fleabag customers.' She eyed him shrewdly. 'But you're not here to discuss my taste in interior design, are you?'

'I shouldn't be here at all, actually. I'm not supposed to be talking to you off the record.'

'But here you are. Guilt, is it?' she asked, with the hint of a smile. 'You used me, didn't you?'

He didn't answer but his face said it all.

'You could have told me, Stefan. I'd have still done whatever you wanted, you know that, surely?' Terri felt genuinely hurt at his lack of trust. 'If it hadn't been for *that*,' she pointed at the black vest hanging over the back of a chair, 'you'd be looking for a new DI, or has Roger Clarke already taken over my office and parked his arse-licking little friend in it?'

'No, he hasn't, and he won't be, not now, so forget that.' He looked down. 'And yes, I told you just enough to whet your appetite. I knew that you'd try to help Sam Helsdown, and I didn't want him out there on his own.' He looked rather miserably into his glass. 'And I wanted you acting totally on your own instincts. If I'd told you what a dangerous, massive, damned horrible case this really is, you'd have started reading things into it, second-guessing every move. I wanted you out there working intuitively, using all the skills that I knew you possessed. And, by the way, I did not instruct you to dive in front of a bullet. We had snipers primed and ready to take those two hoods out the moment they lifted a gun.'

'You were already there? Before I rang in with the location?' Terri shook her head in exasperation. 'What a fool I've been.'

'No, not a fool, Terri, you were an integral part of the whole operation. You gave it authenticity. You were told a little at your earlier debriefing, not much, I know, but I'm telling you now — today, three separate coordinated strikes took place against one of the biggest criminal organisations we've ever come up against. Along with other more powerful departments, we have decimated it, and we have a man we've been chasing for over a decade in custody in an unnamed location. Security services have been after him even longer than that.'

'But the child, Stefan? What on earth did she have to do with anything? I thought I was helping Sam protect his daughter, Zoe!'

He looked contrite. 'I can't say more at present, only that our sole objective in this operation was to recover Sophie. Thanks to you and Sam, she's safe for the first time in her life.'

'Really, I did sweet fuck all. Sam was the hero.' Terri took an angry gulp of her brandy.

'You did more than you think. Okay, we had Julia, our mole, right in the thick of it, and snipers and covert officers on the periphery, but there were a lot of very nasty characters on the move at Saltire Lakes, and I didn't like the odds one bit. That's why I wanted you in there with Sam, his brother and the child. It gave us the edge.'

They sat sipping their drinks for a while, then Terri said, 'I really believed Julia was one of them.'

'She's the best we have, Terri. Well, not us anymore, she's with the security services now. You probably gathered that.'

Terri had a sudden thought. 'How did she know about the bulletproof vest?'

'We, or they, possibly both, know everything there is to know about Sam Helsdown and you, my friend. We certainly knew that you had purchased one, well, two actually, for your drugs raid, but that wasn't covert surveillance on Julia's part, just observation. You're thin as a rake, Terri, with the physique of a marathon runner. Unless you'd put on several stone entirely around your midriff, you had to be wearing body armour. Stabbies can be fairly well hidden, but it's not so easy with the heavy ballistic ones.'

Stefan set down his empty glass and stood up. 'I must go. I only came to apologise, and to tell you I'm hoping that when you hear the full story — and you will — you'll forgive me. You're a brilliant police officer and an exceptional person. I don't want to lose you, or Sam Helsdown, from my station.'

Terri suddenly felt too tired to argue. In any case, if she knew Sam as well as she thought she did, they would both be back in the CID room before too long, no matter what Stefan said. 'Just fill me in as soon as you can, Stefan, I reckon I've earned that much at least. Oh, and call Big Brother off now this is supposedly over. I've never been much of a fan of George Orwell.'

'Agreed on both counts.' He looked concerned. 'Are you really okay after that impact? I almost had a coronary when you went down. I don't like the thought of you being on your own.'

'Oh, sod off, Stefan! I'm fine, and "on my own" is my favourite place to be, so go fret over someone else.'

She watched him go, realising he'd told her just about nothing, bar confirming the fact that she had been the perfect patsy. Oh well. At least he'd had the grace to look contrite, and she had a feeling that those shadowy spooks had probably manipulated Stefan as much as her. When it came down to it, they always seemed to pull the strings.

She ran her bath and stared into the steam rising off it. At least one thing had been clarified. The mystery of Julia. That enigmatic woman was still fighting on the side of the angels. Maybe one day she'd apologise to Sam. He'd been right about her all along.

CHAPTER ELEVEN

It was three weeks before Sam finally got to meet with Julia. Now, wrapped in winter jackets and scarves, they sat huddled on a wooden seat that overlooked the marsh and the silvery cold waters of the Wash. Out in the watery landscape with nothing overlooking them but the sky, they were finally able to say what they had to with only the wind to overhear.

Sam had imagined this meeting a hundred times, along with the wildest reasons why Sophie had been left in his care.

About to hear the truth at last, he felt scared.

They began by speaking about Zoe. Sam had planned to tell Julia about the possibility of buying a house with Mike, so that Zoe would have a proper home to come to when she stayed with him. But he stopped himself, half wondering if there might be a chance they might become a family again. Julia's case was over now. Would she consider coming back to him?

'I thought I'd tell you about Sophie first,' she said. 'Then we could discuss our situation. Is that all right with you?'

God, but she was still so beautiful! Altered, yes. Older, maybe harder, but so, so beautiful. 'Please, go ahead.'

'It all goes back to the case that went so badly wrong. As far as Sophie is concerned, it began right there. A multi-million-pound businessman called Peter Cairns-Smith had his six-year-old son kidnapped and held for an astronomical ransom. He tried to deal with it without involving the police, making the drop himself. The money was duly collected, and his son was left in the allotted place. Only when the desperate father got to the boy, he found him dead. He reinforced his security, but then, six months later, it happened again, with his second son. This time we were all over it like a rash, remember?'

'I can hardly forget,' he said grimly. 'But we failed. The second boy died too. And at that time, the kidnapping wasn't our main concern, we were going after another rich businessman, who had fingers in too many pies to be operating within the law. Nicholas Wentworth: high-flyer, millionaire, entrepreneur and master criminal.'

'And it was when we came to realise that he was behind the kidnapping and murder of the Cairns-Smith children that the whole thing started to unravel.' She hurried him along. 'Forget the details for now, Sam. What you never knew, and few others did either, was that there was a third Cairns-Smith child, a girl called Sophie.' She stared hard at Sam. 'I want you to think what the name Cairns-Smith means to you and tell me.'

He closed his eyes and tried to recall what he'd learned from their investigation, as well as the news reports. 'Dealt in very advanced technology — the serious stuff: artificial intelligence, business automation . . .' He struggled to think of more.

'And the man himself?'

He thought hard. 'Oh yes, he featured on the science forums and even on YouTube. He had an extraordinary talent for . . . Oh.' He let out a breath. 'Mathematics and science. Like Sophie.'

'Like Sophie,' Julia echoed. 'Like all his children, actually, but two were dead. He wasn't going to let that happen to his daughter. He decided that he'd rather lose her early years and have her made safe somewhere a world away than see her die like her siblings.'

'Greece. He sent her to Greece to live with a specially trained couple, Sarah and Darius Lambros. No wonder the villa was well protected, and the child had a tutor instead of going to school.' Poor Sophie. It might have saved her life, but she had been raised amid a web of lies. Even when she thought she'd found her real father, it hadn't been the truth. She would probably spend the rest of her life doubting people and what they said.

'Exactly,' continued Julia. 'Both Darius and Sarah are ex-military, and Sarah is a qualified tutor as well. That villa was Cairns-Smith's brainchild, although it was set up in such a way that it couldn't be traced back to him.'

'And Florence and Jim — oh, and Costas? What of them?' he asked.

'Cairns-Smith didn't want Sophie to grow up in seclusion. He wanted her to have at least some semblance of a family. He put out feelers for suitable candidates and found Florence first. Her family had been killed in an attack on their residence while her father, an eminent diplomat, had been away attending negotiations in Iraq. Baby Florence had been left at home in the care of a nanny and was orphaned. I never found out much about Jim, and even less about Costas, but I think he might have been something of a fly in the ointment.'

Her words left Sam with a rather nasty suspicion that the 'fly' might have been swatted in order to maintain secrecy. 'How is Sophie?' he asked. 'And will I be able see her again? She's an amazing child and I, well, I guess I became pretty fond of her.' Even as he spoke, he knew what the answer would be.

'Sophie is doing very well, Sam. Thanks to you. She has been assessed, and her rehabilitation programme is forging ahead.' She gave him a long look. 'Sophie is set to inherit one of the biggest technology companies in the world. More than that, she is special in her own right. As she matures, her exceptional talents could see her taking that company and its innovations to an even higher level. No wonder Wentworth wanted her and her brothers dead. Cairns-Smith's firm was his biggest competitor and he wanted it brought down. At any cost.'

'And I'll never get the chance to talk to Sophie again, or to say I'm sorry I was part of yet another lie?'

'Sorry, Sam, but she's moved on now. She's out of our hands.'

Julia straightened her shoulders and stared ahead into the watery landscape.

'I'm afraid you're not going to like what I'm going to say, but I did promise to tell you the truth. Please listen and don't interrupt me. This isn't easy for me, you know, and once said, there's no going back. If you ever speak of this again, or question it, you'll come up against a blank wall. But I'm being honest with you.'

Sam saw all his vague dreams of a happy family sink into the chilly waters of the North Sea. He needed to be told the truth at last but he dreaded what she would say.

She began, speaking in a monotone. 'While I was still at school, I was distinguished as having certain attributes that, if developed, might be of use to the intelligence services. I joined in my teens. From that day forward, I swore to abide by our motto: "*Regnum Defende*." To defend the realm, to protect the UK, its citizens and interests, at home and overseas. My life was, and still is, totally committed to that. The security services have been watching Nicholas Wentworth for decades. Because of his power and connections, we have never been able to neutralise him. It has been my mission to trap him, by whatever means. My entire life has centred on that aim, from entering the police force to everything that followed. It has all been part of the operation to bring down Wentworth.'

Sam was stunned into silence. Certain phrases she had used made his blood run cold. What she said next clarified his fears.

'Nothing that happened between us arose by chance, Sam. Everything was planned.'

'Everything?' His voice was choked with emotion.

'It was necessary for me to have a chaotic life. A marriage that failed, as is so often the case in the force, just added to the picture. You were selected as the best option.'

Selected? 'And Zoe? Our daughter?' His voice was unsteady. 'Was she too *selected* as part of the master plan?'

Here, Julia faltered. 'No, that was . . . No matter what you think of me from now on, just know that I love Zoe. I always have.'

It was true she had been a good mother, but was that all a sham as well? A necessary adjunct, designed to make her cover look more convincing?

'When I fell pregnant, it was seen as a serious error of judgement on my part . . .'

Her voice resumed its flat tone. 'But then it was realised that it had strengthened my position considerably. Who would suspect a young mother of infiltrating a major criminal organisation, especially one suspected of supplying arms, weapons and chemicals to foreign powers?'

Sam felt dizzy. The jigsaw pieces in his head began to drift down, one after another, like snowflakes, and slot into place. Every single thing in their lives had been orchestrated by faceless men and women. Their meeting, working together, their affair, their marriage and then their divorce. Even the disastrous case in MIT that had gone so wrong. It hadn't gone wrong at all, it was a smokescreen designed to make Julia look like a bent cop and ease her way into Wentworth's organisation. It had worked too. A picture rose in his mind: Julia flanked by her two 'fellow conspirators'. She had convinced the lot of them, friend and foe.

'What are you?' he whispered, staring across a marsh that had never looked colder or lonelier. 'You're inhuman, a machine, assembled to serve a purpose. There's no heart inside you, just another machine that keeps you functioning. They throw the switch, and off you go. You say you love Zoe, but all you've done is make use of her to make your disguise more authentic. You have no idea what love is!'

She sat for a moment in silence, still looking ahead. 'There is a bigger picture, Sam. In that one, men who kill children and threaten our safety as a nation are brought to justice. In his time, Wentworth has bought and sold life on a daily basis. To bring his corrupt regime to an end, sacrifices had to be made.' She turned and looked at him, her expression impossible to fathom. 'And while we're on the subject of Zoe, I've been given a new assignment. Considering where it'll be located, I believe it to be in Zoe's best interests if she comes to live with you — legally and permanently.' Her gaze was once more on the horizon. 'You will see that she has wanted for nothing, and has been loved and cherished. She speaks of me kindly, Sam, and she is too young to be told anything more just yet. Give her the best life that you can, and you can tell her quite honestly that her mother loves her.'

Julia stood up. 'I have to go.'

Sam remained where he was, looking out at the bleak vista. Well, there was one bright light in all this. Zoe.

As she walked away, he called out, 'And me, Julia? Can I tell our daughter that you loved me?'

No answer drifted back to him on the chilly breeze.

* * *

Julia walked away, her head held high.

Sam never saw the tears that coursed down her face. He never realised that her heart — and yes, she did have a heart — was breaking. He would never know that she had just walked away from the only man she had ever loved.

She would get over it, of course. After all, as Sam had said, she was only a machine, and as she too had stated, sacrifices had to be made.

She quickened her step. She had work to do.

EPILOGUE

Sam Helsdown sat in the arrivals lounge of the airport. Even though he was far too early, he kept his gaze fixed on the gate, wondering what Zoe would look like now. He hadn't seen her in two years, and kids grow up so quickly these days.

He had a distinct sensation of déjà vu, and his stomach churned with anxiety. He pictured Sophie coming through that doorway, a photograph of her 'daddy' clasped in her hand.

He counted down the minutes, until finally it was time.

People flooded through the gates, anxious to meet friends or loved ones, or just to get home again.

A flash of long blonde hair. An eager young face looking this way and that across the concourse.

Their eyes met.

'Dad!' She raced away from her escort and flung herself at him. 'It's so good to be home, Dad! I've missed you so much!' She looked across to the exit and her smile widened. 'And, hey! Uncle Mike! I hope he brought his new car. I've always wanted to ride in a Mercedes.'

'Oh yes, sweetheart, he's got his new toy, but right now, I wouldn't care what he was driving so long as it got us home! And before you ask, yes, I have decorated your room in the exact colours you asked for.' He beamed at his daughter. 'Come on, kiddo, let's go and take a look at your new home.'

THE END

THE JOFFE BOOKS STORY

We began in 2014 when Jasper agreed to publish his mum's much-rejected romance novel and it became a bestseller.

Since then we've grown into the largest independent publisher in the UK. We're extremely proud to publish some of the very best writers in the world, including Joy Ellis, Faith Martin, Caro Ramsay, Helen Forrester, Simon Brett and Robert Goddard. Everyone at Joffe Books loves reading and we never forget that it all begins with the magic of an author telling a story.

We are proud to publish talented first-time authors, as well as established writers whose books we love introducing to a new generation of readers.

We won Trade Publisher of the Year at the Independent Publishing Awards in 2023. We have been shortlisted for Independent Publisher of the Year at the British Book Awards for the last four years, and were shortlisted for the Diversity and Inclusivity Award at the 2022 Independent Publishing Awards. In 2023 we were shortlisted for Publisher of the Year at the RNA Industry Awards.

We built this company with your help, and we love to hear from you, so please email us about absolutely anything bookish at feedback@joffebooks.com

If you want to receive free books every Friday and hear about all our new releases, join our mailing list: www.joffebooks.com/contact

And when you tell your friends about us, just remember: it's pronounced Joffe as in coffee or toffee!

ALSO BY JOY ELLIS

ELLIE MCEWAN SERIES
Book 1: AN AURA OF MYSTERY
Book 2: THE COLOUR OF MYSTERY

JACKMAN & EVANS SERIES
Book 1: THE MURDERER'S SON
Book 2: THEIR LOST DAUGHTER
Book 3: THE FOURTH FRIEND
Book 4: THE GUILTY ONES
Book 5: THE STOLEN BOYS
Book 6: THE PATIENT MAN
Book 7: THEY DISAPPEARED
Book 8: THE NIGHT THIEF
Book 9: SOLACE HOUSE
Book 10: THE RIVER'S EDGE

THE NIKKI GALENA SERIES
Book 1: CRIME ON THE FENS
Book 2: SHADOW OVER THE FENS
Book 3: HUNTED ON THE FENS
Book 4: KILLER ON THE FENS
Book 5: STALKER ON THE FENS
Book 6: CAPTIVE ON THE FENS
Book 7: BURIED ON THE FENS
Book 8: THIEVES ON THE FENS
Book 9: FIRE ON THE FENS
Book 10: DARKNESS ON THE FENS
Book 11: HIDDEN ON THE FENS
Book 12: SECRETS ON THE FENS
Book 13: FEAR ON THE FENS
Book 14: GRAVES ON THE FENS

DETECTIVE MATT BALLARD
Book 1: BEWARE THE PAST
Book 2: FIVE BLOODY HEARTS
Book 3: THE DYING LIGHT
Book 4: MARSHLIGHT
Book 5: TRICK OF THE NIGHT
Book 6: THE BAG OF SECRETS

NOVELLAS
GUARD HER WITH YOUR LIFE

Printed in the USA
CPSIA information can be obtained
at www.ICGtesting.com
LVHW051254220224
772536LV00006B/1203